The Chronicler and Mr. Smith

The Madison Shaw Chronicles
Book One

Angie Martin

This edition published by Angie Martin via Amazon
Text © Angie Martin 2018
ISBN-13: 9781791788469

This book is a work of fiction. Any references to historical events, real people, or real places are used fictitiously. Other names, characters, places, and events are products of the author's imagination, and any resemblance to actual events or places or person, living or dead, is entirely coincidental.

All rights reserved. In accordance with U.S. Copyright Act of 1976, the scanning, uploading, and electronic sharing of any part of this book without the permission of the publisher constitute unlawful piracy and theft of the author's intellectual property. If you would like to use material from this book (other than for review purposes), prior written permission must be obtained by contacting the publisher. Thank you for your support of the author's rights.

Edited by: CJ Pinard

Cover Design by: Amanda Walker
Model: Daniel Rengering
Photography by: Zachary Jaydon

Original Score: Vengeance Divided (Mr. Smith's Theme)
Written by: Christian Goscha
Performed by: Christian Goscha and David Bryant

To learn more about author Angie Martin,
please visit her website at www.angiemartinbooks.com.

This work of fiction contains adult situations that may not be suitable for children under eighteen years of age. Recommended for mature audiences only.

Novels by Angie Martin

Rachel Thomas Novels
False Security (Book 1)
False Hope (Book 2)

Emily Monroe Novels
Conduit
The Darkness (coming soon)

Other Novels
The Boys Club
Chrysalis

Poetry / Short Story collections

Shadows
the three o'clock in the morning sessions

Anthologies

Eye of Fear
The Cat, the Crow, and the Cauldron
Discovery

Dedication

For everyone who has had a dream and made it reality.

For everyone who has stood on the edge and embraced the unknown.

For everyone who has faced down their fears and survived even the darkest of nights.

This book is for you.

Acknowledgements

There are so many people who have made this book possible. Any omissions are entirely accidental.

First and foremost, I have to thank my son, Christian Goscha. I gave you an impossible task: listen to a couple songs that I like and write a song to go with a book you'd never read and knew nothing about. You brought Mr. Smith alive through music and created a theme song for him that cannot be denied as brilliant. Your talent knows absolutely no bounds. You can go anywhere and accomplish anything you dream.

Thank you also to Christian's best friend (my "other son"), David Bryant, for lending your incredible drumming talent to the song.

Johnny and Kailar, you always support me no matter what and without question. I love you both so, so, so much. You, too, Lexi Lulu Buttons, for being my faithful companion through life.

Mom, you're always an inspiration to keep going forward in this crazy dream of being a writer. I love and appreciate you more than you know.

Bree Haack, you are covered in awesome sauce – and thank you also for supporting Christian's dreams. You're a wonderful and vital part of our lives!

Marisa Oldham, life without you would be unbearable. You're not allowed to leave me, never ever. Thank you for helping me come up with some names of characters for this book. Mads loves her nickname; it's absolutely perfect. Now, go publish your next book!

Heather Anne, I've known you only a short while, but you are the "cockiest" author friend I have! I'm pretty darn positive that means you'll be around for a long, long while. Thank you for the intense support and love you've given me.

Leila Kirkconnell, you've always been such a supportive writing buddy and friend. I am so grateful for your guidance, your honesty, and your friendship. I don't ever want to have to navigate this crazy writing world without you!

Amanda Walker, your covers are always amazing, but you outdid yourself on this one. You took my vision, ran with it, and made it into something beautiful. I cannot thank you enough.

Kayla Ries, thanks for being a great friend and helping guide me through the author world with plenty of new ideas and lots of laughter.

Sarah Rutledge, thank you for always being there for me. You are such an awesome friend, and you were amazing at reading as I wrote this. Now that I know how good you are at this, you're in for it!

Prologue

It was strange how my mind processed the odors. I never really thought about it before that night. Never had a reason to. I vaguely remembered something about the olfactory neuron things in the nose inhaling a combination of scents and sending messages up to the brain for translation. This perfect little system that sometimes misinterprets what we think a smell is. And, in that brief moment on that night, I wondered if others in the room smelled the same thing as me.

Curdled milk mixed with rotten raspberries and sour pancake batter. Even now, I can summon the smell to mind, which causes me to wretch a bit before I force myself not to vomit at the aftertaste of those events.

But, that was what I smelled. I noticed it when I entered the building – knew firsthand it could be offensive – but nothing could have prepared me for it, especially in the seconds my mind took to break down the odors into layers. Why would my brain choose that moment? The moment I stared Death in the face, knew he was coming for me – *only* for me – hard, fast, crashing, a thousand teeth shattering against my skin… Or, did my skin shatter in the wake of the teeth? All I knew was that Death had one pristine gold tooth, a luscious red mullet, and a fresh spray tan in mid-January.

And, his muddy green eyes focused solely on me.

Chapter One

Five days earlier...

The solemn winds of winter blew along the line of people, touching the backs of their heads and caressing their faces. It drove their need to shiver in their extra layers, probably chilling their toes to the bone. I sat behind a table, staring up at them, wondering why they would be there. Why give up the luxury of heated homes and blankets to stand in line for hours? I wouldn't do that even if someone was handing out free money, yet, they were in line to part with some of theirs.

"I keep telling the staff to remind them to keep the doors shut." My self-appointed publicist and best friend, Liz Pohl, leaned over my shoulder, her stick-straight blonde hair grazing my cheek. Peppermint hot chocolate-coated breath heated my ear and cheek. "What is wrong with people? Are they trying to freeze you out?"

"Don't worry about it," I said, a permanent smile plastered on my face. "We survived the outdoor book fair in Kansas City in August, right? We can survive anything."

"You won't ever let me forget that, will you?"

"Not until my sunburn finally goes away. Now, I can add frostbite to my list of grievances." I shifted my demeanor from sarcastic to cordial as footsteps approached my table. "Hi!" I said to the woman in front of me.

She looked just like the many before her – a little frazzled, unsure if I was truly a human being, having no idea what to say, but all-in-all excited that a bestselling author sat in front of her. Her trembling hand held my latest novel – released the day before – for an autograph.

I accepted the book and asked, "Who should I make it out to?"

"Eileen," she said. "E-I-L-E-E-N."

"Thanks for spelling it," I said, offering an extra-large smile. I opened to the front of the book and tried to decide what to write. I hated that I couldn't personalize each autograph as I loved connecting with readers, but when so many people were in line waiting, it just wasn't possible.

"May I ask you a question, Miss Shaw?" Eileen asked.

"Call me Madison, please. And, of course."

"In your book, *Withered Flowers*, do you ever regret not writing a happily ever after ending?"

I held my smile in place, though I would have rather gone to the dentist and had all my teeth extracted without the benefit of lidocaine than answer the question. Again. For the millionth time.

"You know, Eileen," I said, ignoring the barrage of curse words running through my mind, "sometimes it crosses my thoughts that I could have gone a different route with that ending." My fingers scratched at the base of my skull, which had been itching for the past couple days. I didn't know what to attribute it to, but at that moment, I believed it to be stress-induced.

"Have you ever thought about rewriting it and releasing it with an HEA?" she asked, her shyness suddenly vanishing as her confidence spiked, as if we were collaborating on the next great American novel. "I was thinking that the book derailed off the HEA path when Heath didn't return Catherine's call immediately in Chapter Six. Maybe if you had…"

HEA. Happily Ever After. The three words in the writing industry I hated the most. In my first novel, *Withered Flowers*, I wrote what I felt was a deeply poetic romance novel without an HEA. Real life didn't always end with the hero and heroine holding hands and strutting down the sidewalk toward a rainbow, serenaded by the playful barks of puppy dogs – at least that was my reasoning. At the time I wrote *Withered Flowers*, I was an independent author – indies, the industry called us – and wanted to write something I loved. Something I could relate to. Something of which I'd be proud.

With my second indie novel, *Sunrise Settings*, I wrote an HEA, against my better judgment. Then, the "right person" read the novel, and before I knew it, I was selling a few thousand copies a day. Agents and publishers started contacting *me*. It was a dream come true… or so I thought.

After my stunning success, my new fanbase read *Withered Flowers*. The reviews were less than favorable. Apparently, I had broken a cardinal rule, committed high treason against the romance genre, not necessarily because I wrote a sad ending, but because I didn't warn readers about it in the book blurb. I didn't even know that was a thing – giving away the ending of a book, divulging whether it would be happy or not before someone reads it. I called that ruining a great read. I never was one to flip to the end of a book after the first chapter. I savored every word, bided my time, and bit off each of my fingernails until I finally read "The End." I thought everyone felt the same way.

I was wrong.

Since then, I had sustained relentless interrogations about the ending of *Withered Flowers*. There was even a website dedicated to my butchering of the ending. Thousands of fan fiction works had flooded the Internet in an attempt to rewrite history. All the while, I wanted to scream at everyone that *I* was the writer. I could write endings the way the characters dictate, and besides that, the characters weren't even real!

Eileen didn't seem to care about any of that as she continued her dissection of my finest work. "Then, Heath could have met Catherine at the diner in Chapter Twenty-four, and—"

"You know, I was actually thinking that I could revisit my other novels and take them in the opposite direction."

"What, uh... what do you mean?"

"Oh, just a little murder here and there. Some blood, guts, criminal masterminds, maybe a chainsaw, and yeah... murder."

The look on her face was as if I had threatened the lives of real human beings, and I instantly regretted my sarcasm. Even though I really meant it. If I could kill all my HEA characters, I would.

Unfortunately, poor Eileen didn't seem to like that at all.

I laughed and shrugged. "I'm just kidding."

Her hand flew to her chest, and she let out a nervous chuckle. "Oh, I see. Yes, funny."

"These are all wonderful suggestions you've given me," I said to her as gently as possible. "I will definitely take them under advisement should I revisit *Withered Flowers* someday."

She looked like I'd just told her I was naming my firstborn after her. "I'm so glad to help. I've always thought of writing myself—"

"I think you should pursue that." I put on a disappointed expression. "I'm so sorry, but I have to get to the next person."

She peeked over her shoulder as if she had forgotten where we were – in the middle of a large bookstore in New York City in mid-January with a line out the door. "I didn't mean to hold up the others. It's just always been a dream to meet you and talk to you about your novels and..." Her eyes lit up brighter than Times Square. "Maybe I can email you personally? Write down my suggestions and—"

"Sure! I'd love to hear from you! The email address is on my website."

"Oh, okay. I'll do... that... tonight." Her forehead wrinkled with the disappointment in her tone, causing me a twinge of regret. But, I couldn't give out my personal email address to every reader.

"Thanks so much for coming in!" I said as she retreated from my table. My cheeks ached from so much fake smiling.

It wasn't that I didn't appreciate readers like Eileen, and I would have hated to ever sound ungrateful, but there was something easier about *not* being a famous romance novelist. I could work my craft the way I wanted to. I could dabble in any genre I wanted. I wouldn't have felt the need to please everyone. I wouldn't have had to apologize for *Withered Flowers*. And, I would have been a far better writer for it. I longed for those days again, even if my royalty checks were so much nicer after my publishing deal.

But, I never stopped loving my readers. Not once.

"Maybe you need a break," Liz said from over my shoulder.

"I'd like to get through a few more first."

"Threatening to kill your characters could get you blasted into the outer stratospheres of Twitter... Whoa, hold on a sec." Before I could process her comments, she stood up and her eyes surveyed the line of readers. "Would you looky there. Who is that?"

My gaze followed hers to the end of the line, where the door had just closed, and I saw the man she referred to. It was unusual for any man to attend one of my book signings, but occasionally one would. But, a man who looked like that... that *never* happened.

"Am I seeing things?" she asked. "Did he just jump out of one of your books and come to life?"

I chuckled under my breath and tried not to stare at the man. Liz was always looking for Mr. Right Now, and it seemed she had found him again. Of course, I couldn't really blame her. His sea-blue eyes seemed to shine from across the room, and the dark hair and few days' growth on his jaw didn't hurt any.

I internally rolled my eyes at myself. Next thing I knew, I'd be thinking about chiseled features and sliding my hand across rock-hard abs. Those things only occurred in my novels. Thankfully.

The crazy need to scratch the base of my skull just above the hairline overcame me again, and my hand flew to the back of my neck to cure the itch. For the past two days, I'd noticed myself scratching more and more back there. It had started out small, but quickly became relentless. I tried putting cortisone cream on it, tried dandruff shampoo, tried popping more than a few Benadryl, but nothing worked. Worse yet, it was hidden beneath my mass of unruly, cinnamon-colored hair. I'd have to shave off a good portion of the thick strands to try to see the rash in a mirror.

The next several readers went through the line without saying anything noteworthy. On average, one out of every ten readers brought up *Withered Flowers*, so I was grateful that sixteen readers passed without uttering the book's name.

Just as I was ready to call for a break, the man who had caught Liz's eye stepped up to the table. He shifted the book from under his arm and placed it in front of me. *Withered Flowers*. I waited for him to tell me his wife or girlfriend ranted and raved on a daily basis over my inability to give the book a happy ending.

He didn't say a word as he slid the book across the table.

"Hi there," I said, my usually chatty demeanor disappearing. "Who should I make it out to?"

"Garrett." He clipped the end of his name, as if he didn't care much to be there. Yet, he had purchased the book, languished through the stinging cold of the morning while waiting in line for my autograph… and it was for *him*, not a girlfriend or his mom or whoever. Definitely not a wife. A cursory check of his left hand revealed no wedding ring.

I scribbled out a generic greeting, signed my name, and passed the book back to him, all with my smile in place.

He accepted the book, opened it to the first page, read the inscription, and closed it. My smile fell at the odd behavior; I couldn't remember a single time when someone reviewed what I wrote in front of me. I watched as his gaze crawled up my face and locked onto my eyes.

The itch on the back of my head attacked me, more intense than it had been since it started. My arms and hands tensed up to resist the urge to scratch, but the itch dug in deeper and wouldn't let go. I casually raised my left hand and acted as if I were straightening up my hair, letting my short fingernails rake across the spot. It provided zero relief. Instead, the action seemed to anger my skin even more. If that were possible.

"Thank you, Ms. Shaw," he said, his voice steady, almost monotone. Then, he walked away.

I stared at his icy retreat through the bookstore. As soon as he left the store, the itching ceased.

Liz jumped into the chair next to me and cleared her throat. Her sympathetic amber eyes watched me carefully, as if I were under observation in a hospital. Or, a mental institution. "Um, Mads," she said, using my affectionate nickname reserved for my closest friends, "you seem to be struggling a bit here. I think it's time for that break."

I turned my attention back to the front door of the bookstore, as if I expected Garrett to waltz back in. Something about him…

Something—

"Mads?"

I looked at Liz to find her hand on my shoulder in a caring gesture. I had almost forgotten she was there. A small itch started at the back of my head again, and I wanted nothing more than to get out of the store, where the air was much too thick and the walls seemed a bit closer to us than before.

"Um, yeah," I said before she could worry about me further. "Let's take that break now."

Chapter Two

The cozy café Liz had chosen for my pre-scheduled interviews with journalists was basically empty when we arrived at 3:15 p.m. We headed to the deserted backroom that Liz had reserved, passing plastic vine-covered, white lattice work randomly placed on the walls between paintings of botanical gardens and tea time outings.

My rumbling stomach wanted to sneak in a quick bite to eat, but my first interview was scheduled at 3:30 p.m., leaving me only fifteen minutes to warm my frozen insides with an incredible cup of lavender mint tea.

Liz raised her coffee mug to her lips, covering most of her freckles. As much foundation as she used, she could never make them disappear entirely. Her natural hair was auburn and as frizzy as a poodle, but she ensured her hairdresser used the lightest hydrogen peroxide blonde possible, and then Liz spent hours each morning with a straightener. She'd been obsessed with hiding her Irish heritage since long before we met. The only reason I knew her secret was one whiskey-filled weekend with her mom and a plethora of embarrassing photo albums.

After sipping the steaming liquid, she said, "See? We survived a whole day of winter in New York City."

I eyed her with a bit of spite. "Who's saying we survived? We don't leave until Monday."

"You'll be fine. All that Midwestern blood in you makes

you easily able to handle a couple snowy days."

"I haven't had that Midwestern blood for five years now," I said, rubbing my hands on the still-warm teacup. "It's all thinned out and gets cranky when the temperature drops below sixty degrees."

She raised her eyebrows and smiled. "We're spoiled by San Diego weather, aren't we?"

Knowing we were running out of time before my first interview, I asked, "Who's up first?"

She lifted the briefcase she usually had surgically sewn to her hip and rifled through her paperwork. She slid on her reading glasses, pulled out a piece of paper, and studied it. "Looks like we have Stone Smith."

I choked on a bit of tea. "I'm sorry. 'Stone Smith?' That has to be the most made-up name I've ever heard."

"That's what I thought, too. Probably an alias, but he runs a small-time book blog here in New York City. Read by a few thousand people." She lowered her glasses and stared at me over the purple rims. "I know how much you love talking to the smaller publications."

Despite Liz's sarcasm, I did enjoy it. I started out small myself, and I always wanted to help others where I could. I wished I could mentor every beginning author in the world, but since that wasn't feasible, I tried to keep my roots in place by communicating frequently with readers on social media. Smaller publications and blogs wanting to interview a New York Times' bestselling author always received an immediate "yes" from me. Even if Liz thought they wasted my time.

I glanced at my watch and noticed we only had a few minutes left until "Mr. Smith" arrived. I snatched the list of interviewers from Liz's hands. At her confrontational glare, I said, "Time for you to vacate the area. I'll look at the rest after our Mr. Smith is done." I hated having anyone else around when I did interviews. The last time she sat in one with me, she answered all the questions before I could say a word.

She pushed back her chair and grabbed her coffee. "Good luck," she said. "I'll be at the bar, not drinking more coffee."

"There's no bar in here," I said.

She pointed to her right and flashed a sardonic grin. "Next door. Have fun with Mr. Smith!"

I shook my head and turned my attention to the schedule. Liz had been busy before we arrived, I noted, as I scanned the names of the journalists. The long list would keep me busy until well after society-established dinner times.

A man clearing his throat caused me to look up from the paper. I opened my mouth to greet Mr. Smith, but stopped when I realized it was the man from the bookstore, Garrett, standing in front of me.

"Ms. Shaw," he said, forcing politeness in his voice. "I believe we have an appointment."

"Um… yes, yes, we do," I said, as he pulled out the chair in front of me and sat down. "You can call me Madison, but I'm not quite sure what to call you."

"What do you mean?" he asked.

My eyes narrowed. "Earlier, you had me make out your book to 'Garrett,' but you scheduled this interview under an apparent alias."

"I never said my name was Garrett. Garrett is my cousin," he said, as if I should have known. "He's a big fan. His wife, not so much."

I took the hidden insult for what it was: this man did not like my work. Not that I expected everyone to fawn over every word I wrote, but something about Mr. Smith burrowed under my skin, crawled across my body, and actually made me itch. Particularly, at the back of my neck.

I resisted the urge to scratch my neck and all the other areas where I was sure hives were popping up as my annoyance increased. Instead, I whipped up my biggest smile and stared into those blue eyes, intent on starting over. "Well, it's nice to meet you, Mr. Smith. My publicist says you run a blog here in the city?"

"Sure," he said, with no hint that he ever planned on starting the interview.

"Did you, um, have some questions for me this

afternoon?"

Unlike most journalists, he didn't move to get a notepad or a Dictaphone. He didn't turn on a recorder on his phone or do anything else that was typical of these interviews. "I do have some questions," he said, leaning back in his chair. "How long have you been writing? Not professionally, just writing in general."

I digested the remedial question, the answer to which anyone with an Internet connection could find on my website. I wondered how long he had been working as a blogger. Liz had said he had a few thousand readers, but I couldn't understand how he obtained them by conducting interviews like this.

"I've been writing my entire life," I said, trying to keep up the appearance of enjoying the interview. "I wrote down my first short story at age nine, but had been telling stories for a few years before that."

"Do you also read romance novels, or do you prefer other genres?"

"Well, of course I read romance, but I also read other genres."

His left eyebrow shot up. "Like what?"

I squirmed in my seat at the uncomfortableness of the question. It seemed innocuous, but the inquiry dug into me, as if he were searching for something specific.

"I, um, I don't... I'm not sure."

"What genre is the book on your nightstand at your house right now?"

I flinched, and my heart beat out of sync. "How do you know I have a book on my nightstand?"

"You said it in an interview last week."

My mind scoured my memory, and, sure enough, I had said that. Not just alluding to it, but I used those exact words. Maybe Mr. Smith was a journalist-type after all. He had certainly done his research on me.

Waving my hand, I let out an airy chuckle, anything to dismiss my accusatory question. As if the man had really been stalking me – what was I thinking? With those eyes, I was sure he'd never had to stalk a woman in his life. *Then again*, my cynical side said, *Ted Bundy was pretty damn good looking, at least until he started killing women.*

Clearing my throat and all the crazy thoughts from my head, I said, "Yes, yeah, I do have a book on my nightstand. It's a horror novel." I bit my tongue as soon as I revealed the genre. I should have lied and said romance. Liz always told me lie about these things to make readers happy, but I had never fared well in the deception department.

"Horror, huh? What's your favorite? Serial killers, the boogeyman, or ghosts?"

"All of the above," I said, a little more relaxed in my tone. "What else is there to be afraid of?"

"Oh, nothing," he said. "But, don't you ever wonder if there are other monsters out there besides the boogeyman and ghosts?"

Other monsters? What was he talking about? Those were the only things that went bump in the night, at least according to every horror book, movie, or television show I'd ever devoured. "I don't believe in the boogeyman or ghosts to begin with, so no. Nothing out there besides some very scary people. What else could there be?"

"Just my curiosity. Next question. Are you writing in the genre you want to?"

The sudden jump in topic caught me off-guard. No one had ever asked me that before, and I didn't know whether to be honest about my aspirations of leaving romance forever, or to lie to keep my readers happy. I settled for in between.

"Yes," I said, "but I wouldn't mind trying my hand in other genres in the future."

"Because Garrett tells me that *Withered Flowers* is an amazing book, but that you kind of went off the rails after you signed your publishing contract. He thinks you sold out as a writer by switching to pure romance novels and not writing another *Withered Flowers*."

Any sense of niceties and keeping up appearances flew

from my mind with his harsh words. I knew my novels after *Withered Flowers* were not great, but who was this man to tell me that? Yet, something else bothered me more.

"You've not read any of my books, have you, Mr. *Smith*?" I accentuated his name to punch home that I knew it wasn't real, but it didn't faze him.

"I haven't," he said. "I don't plan to, either. Not much for trashy romance novels."

The irritation bubbling inside of me spread like a fast-acting virus. "Then, why the hell are you here? Is this how you treat all authors you interview?" I realized that my hand was at the back of my neck, scratching like a madwoman. I pried my fingers away from the sore spot and forced my hands into my lap.

"Been itching for a couple days now, huh?" he asked.

My tightened jaw slacked at his words. "How did you…" I shook my head and let out an incredulous laugh. "Is this a restraining order situation?"

"I'm sorry?"

"Like, where I need to get one." I relaxed in my chair and folded my arms. "Because I've only had one stalker before, and one a lot prettier than you. To be fair, it was a woman, but—"

"This isn't a game, Ms. Shaw." He glanced around the empty back room, as if ensuring no one had filtered in unnoticed, then his intense gaze focused on my eyes. "I don't want to be here any more than you, but I have a job to do."

Confusion filled my mind, almost replacing my anger with him. "And, what 'job' would that be, Mr. Smith, because it certainly isn't running a blog and interviewing an author for whom you clearly have contempt."

"I need to take you with me."

"What?" I came close to jumping out of my seat at his words.

"You're in danger, and the longer you stay here—"

"The only one I seem to be in danger from is you," I said, the seriousness of his veiled threat sinking in. My heart thrust against my ribcage, and clamminess claimed my skin. I pushed back my chair and rose to my feet. "You need to leave."

He stood up as well and crossed his arms, but didn't move beyond that. "I know you don't understand, but let me explain. The itching on the back of your head, it's going to lead them right to you."

I leaned over and retrieved my cell phone from my purse.

"It will start burning, probably later tonight," he continued, "and then they will find you. I need to take you with me—"

"The only thing you're going to do is leave before I call the police," I said, holding up my phone.

He held both hands up as if surrendering. "There's no need to involve the police."

"You came in here, pretended to be a blogger for an interview, insulted me, and then threatened me. Why *wouldn't* I call them?"

"I'm not threatening you…" He clamped his mouth shut and shook his head. "You know what, fine. I am not the best at this."

"At what? Being a normal human?"

"I really can't keep this up with you." He pulled a business card out of his front pocket. "When the burning starts, call me immediately if you want to survive the night."

Before I could say another word, he exited the backroom and disappeared from my sight. Astonished by the exchange, my numb body dropped back into the seat. I ran everything we had said through my mind once more, just to make sure I hadn't misconstrued anything, and then dialed Liz on my phone.

When she answered, I said, "Cancel the rest of the interviews."

"What? Why would you want to do that?" Her voice rose in pitch with every word.

"Please, just come get me and then make the calls."

Something in my tone must have made her understand I wasn't joking. "Okay," she said. "I'll be right back over, and then I'll get them cancelled for you."

"Thank you," I said, ending the call. It was only when I glanced at the business card – which contained a solitary phone number in the middle of the white rectangle – that I realized I was scratching the back of my head again.

Chapter Three

*B**een itching for a couple days now, huh?"*
En route to our hotel with Liz at the helm, headlights from slow-moving cars glared on our windshield as she battled traffic. Red lights, honking horns... it all seemed amplified by the steady snowfall around us. The rental car puttered at an unbearably slow rate of speed, on pace with a golf cart, if even that fast.

Though my writer's brain took it all in, my mind remained fixated on my itching neck. Mr. Smith's question about it haunted me more than anything else he said. The itching had started two days earlier – almost to the hour. The first time I noticed it, I had been packing for my early-morning flight to New York City.

How could Mr. Smith have known about it?

I remembered that Mr. Smith had been at the book signing. I had scratched the back of my head while there – but had he been there to see it? It was possible he stalked me prior to the book signing while I was sightseeing with Liz. I wouldn't have even recognized someone I'd known for life in the overcrowded city, let alone him. I had been too focused on my book signing.

"He really got to you, didn't he?" Liz asked. "What exactly did he say?"

I glanced at her and returned my gaze to the passenger side

window. "I don't want to talk about it. I just want to get to the hotel, pour a glass of wine, and climb into a hot bath."

Liz groaned softly. "I think we need to call the cops."

"And, tell them what? That some guy used a fake name – twice – to schedule a faux interview with me? Nothing he said could be construed as a direct threat. We don't know who he is or where the police could search for him."

"We have his phone number, email, and website he gave when he scheduled the interview."

"It's all fake," I said. Before Liz arrived to pick me up, I had looked up the website on my phone to find it no longer existed. I had also checked his phone number on the sheet against the one on the business card. They didn't match.

The business card...

It wasn't a lot to go on, but I could at least look up the number when I got to the hotel.

I reminded myself that even if the number led me to a name online, I had no crime to report. The police wouldn't do anything about a strange guy scheduling a fake interview. There was nothing left for me to do but go back to the hotel and try to rest.

"The hotel!"

My exclamation startled Liz, who jumped in her seat. "The what?"

"If he's stalked me since I arrived here, he could know what hotel we're staying at."

"All the more reason to call the—"

"Will you just do me a favor? Let's go into the hotel like we normally would, but then leave through the back. We can grab a cab and head somewhere else to stay tonight."

Stopping at a red light, Liz turned to face me. "Are you crazy? We don't have our bags or—"

"We'll call the concierge. He was totally flirting with you. I'm sure he'd arrange for our bags to go to the new hotel."

"So, you won't call the cops, but you want to do all this cloak and dagger stuff?" She shook her head. "Sure, why not? Life isn't exciting enough as it is."

I rested my hand on her forearm. "Thank you so much, Liz. I promise I'll make it up to you tomorrow."

A smile cracked her otherwise solemn expression. "Shopping?"

"You know it," I said, grinning back at her. "All day, if that's what it takes."

"Cloak and dagger it is."

Chapter Four

The new hotel Liz found for us was more to my liking than the modern work of art we stayed in the night before. Bricks comprised the historic building that housed the Westchester Hotel. Far less ostentatious décor – clean, sleek, minimal – filled the lobby. I preferred simplicity to luxurious surroundings, even though the cost of our stay remained the same.

We stopped for dinner on the way to the new hotel, giving the concierge of the old one plenty of time to have our luggage delivered. I tipped him twice as much for the helpful and fast service and retired to my room. Our last-minute reservation forced Liz to stay in the only other available room on the second floor. She opted for that room versus my suite on the top floor. Something about the chi of that room being more favorable for her. I didn't argue.

In my room, I unpacked my suitcase and readied myself for bed. I desperately wanted a bath to relax after my exasperating day, but with a deadline from my publisher looming, I opted instead to work on my next book. I long-ago learned that a book tour was the best time to squeeze in some precious writing time.

As soon as I reached for my laptop, my cell phone rang. The ringtone belonged to my parents, and I cringed inside. With everything that happened during the interview with Mr.

Smith, I had forgotten to call them. With my fingers crossed that Mom wouldn't ream me too much, I answered the phone.

"Madison," she said. "I was starting to worry that something happened to you. You were supposed to call me right after your event ended."

"I'm fine, Mom. I just got caught up in my schedule today."

"You can't do that to us, you know. That city is such a dangerous place to be. I just hate it when you go there. We don't know if something's happened to you, or…"

We went through the same routine every time I stayed in New York. No other city I visited concerned her as much. Even Los Angeles was a breeze compared to the perils of the Big Apple.

"Honey!" my mom said on her end of the phone. "Madison's on the phone!"

I plopped down into the living area recliner and sighed. Depending on the day, it could take anywhere up to five minutes to get my dad on the phone.

"Did you hear me, Roger?" my mom called out. Then, into the phone, she said, "Holly's getting bigger, you know. From the way she's carrying low, I just know it's a boy."

Holly had married my older brother, Miller, six years earlier. She was a doll of a girl, petite, barely over five feet tall, and six months pregnant with their third child.

"Are you going to be back from your trip by the time the baby comes?" my mom asked.

I wanted to tell her for the umpteenth time that I wasn't on a trip; it was a book tour – my job. Instead, I said, "I wouldn't miss it."

I rose from the chair, wandered into the kitchenette, and pulled out a paring knife from the drawer. When we had arrived at the hotel, I had snatched a couple lemons from the bartender downstairs for my water. Cutting them up would provide a nice distraction from my mom's rants and lectures.

"Well, I hope you're right." Her tone of voice vocalized her doubts, justifiably so due to my many flakes on plans to visit home. "Sometimes your trips last so long—"

A click on the phone indicated my dad had picked up the other line. "Magpie! How is your tour going?"

"It's good, Dad," I said, setting my phone down on the counter and pushing the speaker button. The knife sliced through a lemon. "We leave New York in two days and start heading down the coast."

"I saw you on that morning show yesterday," he said. "You did good. Really handled those questions well."

I smiled at my always supportive dad. "Thanks."

"I thought she looked tired." My mom never resisted chiming in with her opinion. "I was just telling her about Holly and the baby. Madison, when are you going to settle down? Maybe it's all these trips you take. You're never going to find a good man who will put up with all that traveling."

I rolled my eyes and worked away on the lemon, cutting it into smaller pieces than needed.

"It shouldn't be hard to find a husband," she continued. "You've got perfect birthing hips, and men look for things like that. You only need three things in life: birthing hips, good breasts, and strong shoulders. But, you have two out of three, so you should be fine."

The paring knife cut into my index finger. I yanked my finger up and stuck it in my mouth, stifling a yelp. The metallic tang of blood coated my tongue as I surveyed the red all over my perfectly good lemon and contemplated my mom's assessment of her only daughter. Larger hips and smaller breasts. My apparent legacy, according to Mom. At least she thought I had adequate shoulders.

"LeAnn," my dad said, addressing my mom. "I think the cookies are burning."

"Oh, my!" she said. "Love you, Madison. Call me tomorrow." She hung up her receiver before I could respond.

"Thank you for saving me yet again," I said to Dad.

He chuckled, and I could envision him shaking his head. "Your mom means well, Magpie."

"I know, but it doesn't make her any less overbearing."

"She just wants you to be happy. Of course, her idea of 'happy' is much different than ours."

Dad knew me too well. We were always close, while Mom and Miller were joined at the hip. Miller was always the one to please her, too. The perfect son: a medic in the Army, a pediatric cardiothoracic surgeon as a civilian, married to a beautiful woman who used her tiny birthing hips the right way. Mom still wasn't sure if being a romance author was a real career. Not that I didn't love my mom – and Miller and I were as close as siblings could be, so I wasn't jealous of his standing with her. I just wished she was a bit less demanding of my "womanly duties," as she called it.

I wrapped a strip of paper towel around the still-gushing wound on my index finger. "I'll settle down eventually," I said, "but I'm only twenty-eight. My career is more important to me right now. In a few years, I'll be established enough that I can be pickier with how many book tours I go on."

"You have eight books out already," Dad said. "I think you're pretty well established. And, your fans love you. Don't be so hard on yourself, but you also have to balance your life. Now, I'm not saying rush out and find someone to marry, but if you need a little time off for yourself, take it."

He was right. He always was. The past six years had taken its toll on me, jetting around the country – and sometimes out of it – to meet with readers, partake in interviews, and trying to keep myself relevant as an author. I needed to sit still long enough to find me, as cliché as it sounded.

"I'm not saying this to guilt you into anything," he said, "but we haven't seen you in over a year. I know you were sick with that flu bug over Christmas, and that's not your fault, but we miss you. We never know what might happen tomorrow, and, well, it would be wonderful to see you more often."

Though he said he wasn't trying to guilt me, regret for not seeing them more filled my soul. "Maybe after this tour is done, I'll come out there for a few weeks."

"That'd be nice to have you home for a bit."

There were a thousand things I wanted to say in that

moment, each one of them on the tip of my tongue, but the only thing that came out was, "I love you, Dad."

"I love you, too, Magpie. Give us a call tomorrow."

I disconnected the call, but lingered for a moment in the kitchenette, still holding the phone. I hadn't realized a year had passed since I'd last visited my family. Life had taken hold of me and made me think there were far more important things than my loved ones. Standing there, I made a promise to myself to rectify that and to never go more than a few months without visiting home, no matter where my career took me.

My cut finger throbbed under the paper towel bandage, so I removed it to assess the damage. The wound had stopped bleeding. I tossed the bloody towel in the trash along with the tainted lemon and wandered back to the bedroom to do some writing. The itching at the back of my head nagged at me once more, followed by a new sensation: burning. Though slight at first, it soon bored deep inside, as if a laser sliced through my skull.

I stopped next to my bed and dropped my hand away from my burning skin. Mr. Smith had said it would burn, and that I should call him when it started. I grabbed my purse off the dresser and rifled through it until I found his unusual business card. As I picked up my cell phone off the bed to call him, I realized the ridiculousness of it all. There was no possible way he could have known it would burn. He saw me itching at the book signing and again at the café, and he used that to get to me. I probably experienced the burning as a psychosomatic response to his suggestion. My subconscious always worked overtime, my overactive writer imagination filling in blanks where it could.

I didn't know what his angle was. Why would he be deceitful and pseudo-threatening? No matter his intentions, I didn't want to indulge his potentially dangerous delusions. I threw his card in the trash can next to the bedside table and climbed into bed, where I could dive into my imaginary world and leave Mr. Smith far behind, despite my burning scalp.

Chapter Five

My eyes flickered open, and I yawned audibly. My sight adjusted to the darkness, and the lack of light around the balcony door informed me it was sometime in the middle of the night.

I pushed myself up from the bed into a sitting position and looked around the room. Another yawn controlled my mouth, drowsiness not letting go of me quite yet. I sighed and spotted my laptop next to me on the bed. I often woke up next to my laptop after a long night of writing, and its presence comforted me. Unlike other women who preferred the company of a man, my laptop reminded me of my only purpose in life: writing.

Sliding out of bed, my bare feet sunk into the cold carpet, and a shiver raced through my body. My toes sought out my cozy slippers and found them next to the bedside table, right where I had left them.

I stuffed my feet into the slippers and zombie-shuffled to the bathroom. My thoughts picked up where I left off in my writing before falling asleep, and I mentally worked on an issue with my plot's timeline. After using the restroom, I decided to open my laptop for a few more minutes to finish the scene. I didn't have to be anywhere until nine in the morning, so a little more work wouldn't hurt.

As I walked into the bedroom, the burning in the back of

my head started up again. I reached for it and tried to massage the pain away, but it had no effect. A chill breezed through the room, and I stopped short before reaching the bed. Squinting my eyes, my heart racing, I crept toward the balcony door. It was ajar, the wintry night air pushing through the slight crack and driving straight into my soul.

My gaze traveled to my bedroom door, which was also open. I had shut it prior to going to bed. Staring at it, wondering how it opened while I slept, I heard a noise in the living room area.

Someone was in my suite.

I tried to control my ragged breaths and think through my situation. The only exit from my suite was in the main hallway, past the kitchenette, off the living room, but I couldn't run through there without whoever had broken in seeing me. I could scream and pray someone came to my aid, but my suite was the only room on the top floor. By the time someone on the floor below me heard my cries, it would be too late.

What to do, what to do? My frantic mind panicked in the moment, but one small part still ran on logic.

Call for help.

With light footing, I made my way back to the bedside table. I picked up the telephone receiver and dialed 911. No ringing. I clicked the hook switch several times, but no dial tone sounded, even when I pressed zero for the hotel's front desk.

My trembling limbs threatened to slow me down, but my brain worked overtime on how to get to safety. *My cell phone.* Where had I put it? I remembered leaving it at the end of the bed, but I didn't touch it after that. I moved to the front of the bed, and my hands traveled across the messy bedspread, but I couldn't find it. I dropped to my knees and searched the floor in case it fell off while I slept, but I came up empty.

I froze at the prickling of hairs on the back of my neck. A sensation of not being alone in the room overwhelmed me. I opened my mouth to scream for help, but a hand clamped down over my lips, shutting me down before anything could escape.

"Don't scream," the gruff voice whispered. "Stand up slowly."

Terror pounded through my veins, and I did as the man ordered. His arm wrapped around my waist as soon as we stood. He held me close against his body, his calloused hand still covering my mouth.

"I need to know you're not going to make a sound," he whispered in my ear.

I nodded my head, with no intention of following his instructions. I'd rather die screaming my head off and clawing my way to safety than to stand still and let him kill me, kidnap me, or – God forbid – rape me.

As if reading my thoughts, he said, "I'm not going to hurt you, but there are others coming who will. I need to get you out of here."

With his last words, I recognized the voice. *Mr. Smith*. His earlier statements in the café weren't empty threats after all. He had come there to kill me.

Adrenaline surged through my body. I wiggled and squirmed and fought him with everything I had, but he was much stronger than I could have imagined. Still holding me tight, his chest muscles contracted against my back while his arm tightened around my waist, giving me the full scope of his strength. I would never get away from him like this. Maybe, I couldn't get away from him at all.

My fatigued muscles surrendered, and I collapsed against him. My brain hadn't given up on escaping, but my body refused to respond to any commands.

"Don't try anything stupid," he said, annoyance lacing his words. He let go of my mouth, and his arm circled my chest, binding my arms to my body. "I told you to call me as soon as the burning started."

I had only met him earlier that day, but for some strange reason, he brought out the sarcastic, bitter side of me – even after breaking into my suite. Through gritted teeth, I said, "I make it a habit not to call potential kidnappers and murderers."

"I'm not the one you have to worry about."

My eyes widened. "What do you mean?"

"They're heading up here right now. I'm going to release you, but I need you to do as I say if you want to survive this."

That was the second time he used that phrasing, but my mind had shifted from being afraid of him to terrified of whoever might come into the suite next.

Mr. Smith loosened his hold on me, but kept one hand on my waist and the other on my upper arm. I twisted around to see him, and he adjusted his grip accordingly. His narrowed blue eyes flashed anger and urgency underneath ruffled strands of dark-brown hair.

"Who's coming up here?" I asked, my voice barely above a whisper in case "they" could hear me.

"Blood seekers." He spoke so matter-of-factly that I almost didn't question him.

Almost.

"Blood... what?" My tone rose as the ludicrousness of his words hit me. "What are you—"

A loud banging came from the door of my suite. I stepped forward and grabbed his shirt in my fists, instinctively seeking protection from the stranger.

"They're here," he said. His fingers under my chin lifted my head until I looked up at him. "Do exactly what I say. We need to get downstairs."

"How?" I whispered. "There's only one door."

"Fire escape." He grabbed my hand and led me to the balcony. "It's the only way."

My gaze traveled over the railing, down to the dizzying asphalt in the poorly-lit alley behind the hotel. My deep-rooted phobia of heights tugged his hand in the opposite direction. "I... I can't. It's too high up and—"

He turned to face me, his stern eyes conveying authority. "It's either heights or torture and death. For both of us."

Out of the depths of insane fear, my sarcastic nature reared up again. "Oh... Well, if you're giving me a choice—"

A crash came from the front of the suite, much louder this time, as if the door had blown inward to let "them" in.

Mr. Smith knelt, dragging me down with him. Crouched down, we moved back inside the room and behind the dresser. He peeked around the door leading from the bedroom to the living area. Out of curiosity, I poked my head around his body. Two large shadows moved across the room, past the bedroom, one of them holding the distinct outline of a gun.

"She's in here somewhere," one of the men said. "I can sense her."

I ducked back behind Mr. Smith, the reality of the situation taking hold of my racing heart. No matter who he was, he couldn't be any worse than the two men in my room. And, at least one of them had a weapon. Just as Mr. Smith had attempted to warn me about that afternoon.

"Check the bedroom," a second voice said.

Mr. Smith turned to me and mouthed, "Stay here." He motioned to the area behind me, indicating he wanted me to hide.

I tiptoed across the bedroom and hid behind the dresser. Crouching, I tucked my body down, making it as small as possible, and forced only shallow breaths into my lungs so the intruders couldn't hear me. A strange odor wafted into my nostrils. Pungent and rancid, it curdled in my stomach, and I fought against the rising bile in my throat.

A loud grunt came from the other room, followed by a heavy thud. I prayed Mr. Smith had gotten one of them from behind. Otherwise, they would be in the bedroom within seconds. More groans and grunts filled the air, with what sounded like heavy footwork and several good hits. With the telltale noises of fighting, it meant Mr. Smith was still in the running to win the battle against the intruders.

I don't know how much time passed with the echoes of the fight surrounding me. I balled up my chilled hands and lifted them to my mouth, trying to focus on warming them with my breath. I rocked back and forth until the fight ceased in the other room. I squeezed my eyes shut, not wanting to know who the footsteps entering the bedroom belonged to.

"Madison," Mr. Smith said.

I shot up to my feet and allowed myself to take a deep breath. Blood dripped from cuts in his cheek and lip. Even though he wore black, the glistening red smeared across his shirt caught my attention. His wounds didn't seem capable of producing that much blood.

"More will come soon," he said. "Let's go."

I didn't argue as he yanked my arm and dragged me outside onto the balcony. The freezing night air bit my skin through my thin pajama bottoms and long-sleeved top. To the left of the balcony, I saw the fire escape stairs. Looking over the edge, they seemed to wind down into a vortex of dark nothingness. With a good three feet between my balcony and the fire escape and nothing to connect the two, my head swirled with the possibilities of all the ways I could fall to my death. A slip on the icy railing, falling through the rusted-out bottom, someone following us outside and pushing me off.

"I'm right behind you," Mr. Smith said. "I won't let you fall. Climb up on the balcony and take one step over to the fire escape."

One step. One little step over to the poorly thought out, rickety-looking fire escape. Twenty stories of dead air between me and the ground – all in that one step.

I grabbed Mr. Smith's outstretched hand and let him help me to the top of the railing. Before I froze up, I took the step to the fire escape. Mr. Smith climbed up on the railing and held my hand until I safely stepped down to the grated floor.

The strange odor hit me again, and I took several quick whiffs to try to identify it. "What's that smell?" I asked Mr. Smith as soon as he stepped down to my level.

"More of them coming. Get down the stairs, now. Don't stop for anything."

I rushed down the first flight of stairs, the second, the third, but stopped when I realized Mr. Smith wasn't behind me. A whoosh from above caused me to lean over the edge and look up. I couldn't see much outside of the two figures battling it out on the narrow fire escape ledge. I ducked back when an object plunged over the side of the top level. Wet drops splattered my face as it passed me on its way down. Though happening quickly, my brain processed it as if it fell in slow motion.

A head.

A severed head.

My breathing and heartbeat halted at the same time. My fingers lifted to my cheek, and I wiped at the dampness. When I pulled my hand away, crimson painted my fingertips.

A hand on my shoulder brought me back to the present. A scream caught in my throat, and I lashed out at the monster behind me. Mr. Smith grabbed my flailing arms and stilled me. My breathing resumed with a gasp. I jumped toward him, leaned into him, and latched onto his hand as if letting go would result in my death.

"A-a head," I said. "That was a head."

His jagged breathing entered my ears, but he made little move to comfort me. Instead, he pushed me away. "You have to keep going." A noise above us made him glance up. "Find Garrett. He's waiting down there for you."

"I can't just—"

"Go!"

His shout rattled me, and then he was gone. Back up the fire escape, holding a machete in an attack stance, leaving me wondering where the weapon came from.

Something inside of me forced my legs to wind down the stairs until I reached the blessed concrete of the alleyway. I glanced around for Garrett, the mysterious cousin, but saw no one.

Headlights flashed in my direction, and I instinctively ran toward them. A tall, blonde woman hopped out of the passenger side of a car when they reached me. "Madison?"

"Where's Garrett?" I asked, surprised I could even form the words with the severed head still tumbling through my mind.

"Driving." She yanked open the backdoor. "Get in."

I didn't question as I climbed into the car. It was either that or going back to the land of falling heads. I scooted over to behind the driver's side as the woman followed me in. She barely shut the door before the car tore down the alley. It swerved right at a dead-end and continued straight for at least a minute.

The driver slammed on the brakes, throwing me against the back of his seat. He turned around and looked at me. "Sorry about that," he said. "Where's Spencer?"

I blinked. "Who?"

"Spencer. My cousin." At my silence, he added, "The man who just came up to get you."

"You mean Mr. Smith?" I asked, still trying to comprehend who Spencer was.

"Yes," the man said. "I'm Garrett. This is my wife, Keira."

I looked at the woman again, not knowing what to say.

"Hey, Madison," she said, a sympathetic smile crossing her lips. "Sorry for all this mess. Did Spence tell you about us?"

"Who?" I asked again, nothing really sinking in. "There was a head… this head just… fell down. And, the blood. The blood on the head was there, and it flew down next to me and…" I knew my words were not making sense, but I couldn't seem to put my thoughts together.

Keira glanced at Garrett. "I think she's in shock."

He handed her something from the front seat, and she turned to me. "You have some blood on your face," she said, holding up a wet wipe.

I couldn't move to take it from her, so she pressed it to my cheek and cleaned me up. Despite my freezing skin, the wipe was surprisingly cool.

"We can't wait much longer," Keira said to Garrett.

"He said five minutes." Peeking at his watch, he said, "And, it's been ten. Damn it! I don't want to leave him."

"We have to go," Keira said. "Her mark is burning. There's only so much time before they find us."

My hand wandered to the back of my head, hoping to stem the pain in my skull. How did this woman know about the burning?

"He'll catch up," Keira said. She accepted something from

Garrett and faced me again.

My gaze wandered down to her hands to find her holding a small cup containing clear liquid.

"I know you're scared," she said. "You've seen some terrible things, and you're in shock right now. I've been in the exact same place as you, so I get it. But, I need you to drink this. It will knock you out, but it's the only way to stop your mark from sending out signals and attracting more blood seekers."

I tried to speak, but nothing came out. Given the choice between drinking an unknown substance from a stranger whose friend had just saved my life and those who broke into my suite and apparently wanted to kill me, the decision was easy. Besides, if Alice could survive drinking strange concoctions in Wonderland, so could I.

I hoped.

She pressed the cup into my hands, helped me lift it to my lips, and tilted it so I could drink. I didn't question, didn't protest, just swallowed the strange-tasting liquid. She took the cup from me and said, "Garrett, we have to go. Spence will get back somehow. He always does."

Serenaded by Garrett's cursing, the car pulled into the street. Watching the passing street signs taking me further away from my hotel – from my comfort zone – my vision clouded over. "Who the hell is Spencer?" I asked again, before giving into the darkness.

Chapter Six

My cozy, extra-plush throw blanket wrapped around my contorted body brought an instant smile to my lips. Safe in my bed at home, the bad dream was nothing more than that. I always slept best at home, in my comfortable bed with a thick pillowtop. My head cushioned by my fluffy pillow, I turned over for a few more minutes of sleep, thankful my long book tour was finally over.

My eyelids cracked open as the events in my hotel suite resurfaced. I never finished my tour. I had no memory of the other stops, of spending time with Liz, laughing and joking. No memory of flying home with her, of crawling into my bed… the bed in which I now laid…

I sat straight up and took in the unfamiliar room around me. My blanket, my pillow, yes… but not my room.

"Where the hell am I?" I asked myself under my breath.

I hopped out of the bed and noticed I was wearing the same pajamas I had on when Mr. Smith broke into my hotel room. My last recollection of the night was the balcony and Mr. Smith holding my hand, helping me over to the fire escape.

I decided to explore my surroundings to try and resurrect other memories. The room was well-decorated, as if someone had put some thought into it. A matching, dark-oak bedroom set filled the room, the walls covered with abstract paintings similar to the ones in my home. Around the same size as my own bedroom, I wandered across the room and found a massive attached bathroom, one large enough to be part of a master suite.

I ventured into the walk-in closet off to the left of the bathroom and rifled through clothing like the ones in my closet. The ones I'd left behind in my home in San Diego. I pulled a plaid, button-up shirt off the rack and saw the small soy sauce stain at the bottom from when Liz and I last ate sushi. I hadn't worn the shirt since that night. These weren't just similar clothes; they were *my* clothes.

As I exited the closet, the bedroom door opened, and a woman walked in. Taller than me with sharp facial features and her blonde hair in a high ponytail, she somehow looked familiar...

"Hi, Madison," she said, offering a genuine, warm smile. "I'm Keira. We met last night."

Keira, I thought as memories flooded my head. A car, a man in the car – *Garrett! Keira's husband*, I remembered. The mysterious cousin that Mr. Smith had me sign the book for.

My head bobbed up and down slowly as I worked through the events of last night. "I remember you. You gave me something to drink to knock me out."

She grimaced. "Not exactly the best way to start off a friendship, huh?" She took a few steps forward. "At least, from what I know of you, I think we'll get along great after you're settled in."

Friends? Settled in? What was she talking about?

"I know this all seems strange to you," she continued, "but I promise, it will all start making sense soon." She sat on the edge of my bed, facing me, and sighed. "I've been right where you are, and I remember being terrified."

Despite my circumstances – not knowing where I was, how I got there, and talking to the woman who drugged me – my gut said to believe her. I didn't know if it was her authenticity, her radiating kindness, or her sympathetic tone of voice, but I trusted her.

Maybe, it was because I was also terrified. It didn't hit me until she said the word, but my nerves reacted accordingly, as if they were stretched-out rubber bands ready to snap. Every muscle in my body quivered, and my mind raced with the possibilities of how this could end.

I sat on the bed next to Keira. "I think I'm ready to go home now," I said. I didn't care much about a book tour, or Liz's scheduled events, or the hundreds of readers I would miss out on meeting. The safety of my house beckoned, walls I could trust, a bed I knew.

Yet, most of my clothing from my home in San Diego filled the closet. Someone had broken into my house to retrieve them and brought them to wherever I was. I wasn't going home.

Before I could ask another question, Garrett came through the door. "Glad you're awake!" he said, his cheerful voice bounding around the room. His dirty-blond, neatly-trimmed hair was in stark contrast to the dark, unkempt, scruff-laden style of his cousin, Mr. Smith. "Has Keira explained everything yet?"

"I was getting there," she said.

"I can't believe it's really you," he said to me, ignoring his wife. "Did she tell you how much I love your work?"

"You... you read romance novels?" I asked, curiosity overriding my other thoughts.

"He loves them," Keira said. "I'm sure I'd love them, too, but I never was much of a reader."

"I thought *Withered Flowers* was amazing," he continued. "Must have read it twenty times by now. Not that I don't like your other books, but there's something about *Withered Flowers*."

Mr. Smith's words from our conversation at the fake interview hit me. "But, you think I 'sold out' after *Withered Flowers*."

"Sold out?" he asked. "Why would I think that? You went in a different direction with your work, but that doesn't mean I don't like the rest of your books."

My head spun between reality and what Mr. Smith had

told me. Between first thinking his name was Garrett, getting the name Stone Smith from him as a fake journalist, then him breaking into my suite... and then a falling head and blood. Nothing about any of it made any kind of sense.

Mr. Smith came into the room, wearing different clothes than he had on the night before, yet appearing even more disheveled. He was the last person I wanted to see, despite him having saved my life, possibly more than once. Of course, if he had never shown up to my book signing, maybe none of it would have ever happened. He was the one who pushed me through the door and into this surreal world, and there he stood. What calamity would he create for me next?

"Oh, good," he said, his eyes focused on me, sarcasm lacing his voice. "You made it. Are you all settled in now? Have a nice sleep? 'Cause I was out there fighting most of the night just so I could get back here and make sure *you* were okay."

"What..." I shook my head. "What are you talking about?" Looking at Keira, I asked, "What did I do wrong?"

Though standing a few feet away, Mr. Smith's figure seemed to hover over me. "Everything. When I tell you to do something, you do it. You don't hesitate. You don't wait. You just do it."

"When did I—"

"On the fire escape." He stared at me for a moment, as if waiting for me to remember. "I told you to keep going. Instead, you stood there, waiting for someone to escort you down each step. Because of you, I got stuck there, and—"

"There was a head!" I yelled, jumping to my feet. "A head. A frickin' severed head fell down right by me!"

"Oh, I'm sorry," he said, crossing his arms to match his condescending tone. "Did you get a little blood on you? I was *covered* in it by the end of the night in a nonstop fight for *my* life while *you* were playing *Sleeping Beauty*."

"Maybe if you did a better job of explaining what the hell was going on, I wouldn't have stopped at the first sign of a severed head, *Mr. Smith*!"

He whirled around and made his way to Garrett. "Yeah,

that's another thing. 'Stone Smith?' Are you kidding me?"

"What?" Garrett asked, shrugging. "She's a romance novelist. I wanted to give you a romance-type name so she'd do the interview."

"Names have nothing to do with what interviews I accept," I said, my anger at all the deception rising. "I don't need a sexy name to talk to a reporter, which the name isn't, and he wasn't. And, by the way, Garrett"—I stuck my thumb out in Mr. Smith's direction—"he's the one who said you thought I sold out as a writer."

Garrett turned on Mr. Smith, much to my satisfaction. "Why would you do that? You know I love her books!"

Mr. Smith focused his narrow eyes on me. "A romance writer. Seriously!" He tornadoed out of the room with Garrett in tow, who pummeled Mr. Smith with questions about what else he had told me.

I looked at Keira for help. Her lips remained sealed, though they formed a large smile.

"What is it with Mr. Smith?" I asked her. "Why is he so irritated with me every time I talk to him?"

"It's not you," she said. "Spencer's been irritated since birth."

I reclaimed my seat on the edge of the bed next to her again, closed my eyes, and pinched the bridge of my nose. That was right. His name wasn't Garrett or Mr. Smith. It was Spencer.

"He'll come around," she said. "He's not big on change, and right now, you're a huge change here."

"I don't even know where 'here' is, or who you people are, or what I'm doing *here*."

"Then, it's probably time for a tour and a history lesson. Why don't you take a shower and get in some clean clothes, Madison?"

"Call me Mads," I said, without thinking. Only my closest friends called me that, but again, there was something about Keira that made me not only trust her, but attracted me to her as a friend.

"Sure thing, Mads." She rose to her feet. "Just come outside when you're ready."

"By the way," I said, "is Spencer really 'Mr. Smith' or does he have another last name?"

"It's Frye. Spencer Frye."

"Hmm," I said, mulling over the revelation of his God-given name. "I think I like 'Mr. Smith' better."

Keira laughed. "I think I do, too."

Chapter Seven

They would never let me go.

The realization dawned on me while I dressed. There had been no hint at captivity or kidnapping; outside of Mr. Smith, I had been met with nothing but kindness and comfort. Between the niceties, the bed, the shower, the provisions in the bathroom, I sensed no threat. Yet, my clothes from my home in San Diego were in the closet and my blanket and pillow were on the bed. That didn't inspire much confidence about allowing me to leave.

Then again, the doorknob to the world beyond the bedroom rotated easily under my grip. They hadn't locked me in the room. When I stepped outside into what could only be described as a lobby, there were no armed guards. Nothing prevented me from roaming free and finding a door to the outside. I also noticed that my fear from earlier had faded. I should have been terrified of my circumstances, but I remained quite calm.

When I glanced up, I spied the security cameras near the ceiling at various intervals around the room. Five in total, all unhidden. Ducking back into my room, I scanned the ceilings for signs of surveillance, but discovered none. At least they weren't watching me sleep or shower.

Who were these people?

I left the room again and took in the setting. The center of the room had couches, a coffee pot, even magazines on side tables and plants in the corners. A waiting room of sorts. I walked to the center of the room and looked up. Five stories between myself and the ceiling, with nothing in the round center. Hallways wrapped around the middle of each level, with columns for support – I could only liken the structure to a hive. I appeared to be on the ground floor, but something told me that other levels stretched out beneath my feet. Nothing about this place seemed normal.

So, why did something about it put me at ease? As if I were... home?

I shook the strange thought away. That combined with my feelings of friendship toward Keira would put me at a disadvantage around my alleged captors – if they could be called that. They *did* save my life.

The sight of Keira walking toward me from one of the alcoves relieved my confusion. Maybe, she would provide me with answers. She had mentioned something about a tour and a history lesson. She had also said that, in the past, she'd been exactly where I was.

"Hey, Mads," she said, a bit of a skip lifting her feet as she strode toward me. "Feeling better?"

"Definitely." A truthful response. Somehow, a hot shower and a fresh pair of clothes had changed most of my outlook on the recent events.

"I figured it wouldn't take long," she said when she reached me. "Your mark must be fully developed now."

I realized I hadn't scratched the base of my skull nor had it burned since I woke up. She had mentioned it earlier, and I assumed it must be the annoying thing on the back of my head. "What is this 'mark?'"

"There are two ways you get here. You're either born into this life or you're called to it. Garrett and Spencer were both born into it. You and I were called. All of us have a mark. For them, developing your mark isn't a big deal, but for those of us who are chosen as adults, it can be alarming."

Chosen? The only thing I had ever been chosen for was

being a writer – and that talent came with enough headaches as it was. "I was chosen? How?"

"Lineage," she said. "The mark can skip hundreds of years, but at some point, back in time, one of my relatives – and one of yours – were part of The Order."

Though mention of The Order raised questions, my brain stuck on the idea of the mark and what it looked like.

As if she read my mind, she turned around and moved her ponytail out of the way. "You can look at mine, though it's hard to see under all the hair."

I stepped up to her and parted the blonde strands of hair, right around the same spot where I had felt my mark. Raised, red lines appeared to create a picture of sorts, but I couldn't tell what it was since I couldn't see the lines all at the same time.

"What is it? What does it mean?"

"It's a way of identifying others like us. When the mark comes in, it means you've been called to duty. But, it also protects you in a way. I came here the same as you, with an itchy, burning skull and no clue as to what was happening. After my mark finished forming, I wasn't as scared anymore. It connected me to the others here and to this place."

Her explanation made a weird kind of sense, but it left me with even more questions. "You said last night something about signals. What are those?"

"The mark is magical, powerful. When it first comes in, it sends out a homing beacon of sorts. It's how we found you, how we find anyone who's called into the life. But, we had to find you before others did."

"Others like the ones who broke into my hotel room? Mr. Smith said they were there to kill me."

"You're extremely important to us and what we do, Mads. Much more important than people like me, Garrett, and Spencer. We have the numbers in our order, but yours... well, there's only fourteen others of your kind in the world. The blood seekers would do anything to get their hands on you. In here, you're safe. Though your mark was still forming while you slept, its signals were weaker with you unconscious, and now that it's formed, it won't send out any other signals. Even if you woke up and it hadn't come in all the way, the signals can't penetrate these walls, so they couldn't have found you."

My eyes seemed to cross as my thoughts spun with the barrage of strange information. "I understood maybe ten percent of what you just said."

Keira chuckled. "I know, it's a lot. But, it will all make sense the more you learn."

I looked up at one of the security cameras, and the idea of being trapped clutched my throat, strangling my emotions. "I'm not going home, am I?"

She sighed, a bit of regret, even empathy blowing out with her breath. "If you leave here now, you're dead within a day. Even though your mark has stopped sending out signals, they still know who you are. You're much too famous to disappear out in that world. They'd find you, fast."

Twinges of pain lanced my heart. "I can't stay here, though. I mean, my family, Liz… Oh, no! Liz! She's probably losing her mind right now. I have to let her know I'm okay. I'm supposed to be at a book signing right now, and—"

"Dead, Mads. You'd be dead, and you might bring death to your loved ones, too."

Dizziness swirled the room around me, and I stumbled back to the nearest sofa. Grasping the armrest with a clammy hand, I landed on the soft cushion, my glassy vision fixated on the floor.

Keira sat next to me and rested her comforting hand on my forearm. "This is the hardest part of this life," she said, her voice barely above a whisper. "I had to go through it, too, and though my family was quite broken, it was still difficult."

"I have to let them know I'm okay."

"You can't. I'm sorry, Mads."

"But, my dad… my dad…" Our conversation from the night before resounded in my mind. Did he somehow know it would be the last time we'd talk?

"We never know what might happen tomorrow…"

He knew. He always had a knack for those things, sensing

the worst of the worst.

Tears brimmed my eyes, but I somehow managed to keep them from spilling over my lids. "You're not going to let me go, are you?"

"We're not keeping you here. You can do whatever you want. Leave at any time." She lifted her hand from my arm and slid back against the couch cushion. "You're not a prisoner."

I swung my gaze toward her. "I don't… I don't understand."

"You will. And, when you do, you won't want to leave. None of us ever do."

"So, I just disappear, and my family always wonders what happened to me?"

"Not exactly," Keira said, standing up. "Let me introduce you to the others and show you around."

Chapter Eight

We started the tour on the main floor, where my bedroom was. There were four other doors in the round lobby, each leading to someone else's bedroom – according to Keira. She pointed down two other hallways leading to additional bedrooms in the front and back of the complex. She also showed me the outlet that contained three elevators.

We took the middle elevator up to the second floor, which Keira explained was the level containing the kitchen, dining area, and a fully-equipped gym.

"How many others are here?" I asked as we left the kitchen.

"There are eight others here like me, but no one else like you." She pressed the up button for the elevator. "There are also two who handle computer technology, one who coordinates and shares information with the other complexes, a chef, and three others in the cleaning and maintenance department. Then, we have two in our medical department, a doctor and a nurse."

"Quite the operation," I said. The elevator door slid open, and I followed her inside. "What do you mean, 'like you?'"

Pressing the button for the third floor, she said, "There are three Orders, and each of us are called into only one of them."

"Orders? Sounds like the Templar Knights or something."

"It is, but we're older than they are by about a couple thousand years, give or take. And, we tackle things the Templar Knights couldn't ever imagine."

Her response caught me off-guard. "What are the Orders?"

"There is The Order, which is where everyone who doesn't fit into the other two fall. That also includes our high council, which oversees all the complexes and our activities. I'm part of the Order of the Night Stalker."

"Night stalker?"

"Fancy way of calling us hunters." She turned left into a room. "Garrett and Spencer are also night stalkers."

Before I could ask any other questions, the computer monitors in the room caught my attention. My author headshot from my most recent book was plastered on one of them, while another contained basic stats about me. My age, place of birth, current and previous residences, medical information, and more. The other screens showed various news stations, a cacophony of overlapping newscaster voices filled the air. Several steps down led to a hub in the center of the room where the two dark-haired occupants of the room, both behind computer screens, typed furiously on their keyboards.

I followed Keira down the steps. She cleared her throat, getting the attention of the other two. When they whirled around in their chairs and saw me, they leapt to their feet, one female, one male. Both were around the same height, just a few inches above my five-foot-five stature. The woman's warm smile reminded me of Keira, though this girl's mass of frizzy, dark curls with the original streak of red tried to burst out of the hair clip holding it back. The man's hair touched his shoulders, framing his unblemished olive complexion.

"You're here," the woman said. "I mean, I know you're here, but you're *here*."

"This is Jiong Chen and Sandra Molina," Keira said. "They are the computer geeks for the complex."

"And, you're the new chronicler," Jiong said, walking toward me. His excited eyes searched my face as if he were inspecting a new toy.

My brow narrowed. "The new what?"

"Chronicler," Keira said. "You belong to the Order of the Chronicler."

"Chronicler?" A huff came out under my breath. "You'd think someone could come up with an easier name to say."

Sandra turned to Keira. "Oh, I like this one."

I stepped past them and stared at the monitor with my information on it. "What is all this?"

Jiong walked up beside me. "This is our current project, which is you. We're working on your cover for disappearing. Right now, there are no media reports of your disappearance. Your publicist filed a police report, but there hasn't been any other movement."

"Liz filed a police report?" My head swirled with thoughts of her worrying about me. "I've been pretty open to everything," I said to Keira, "but I have to let her know I'm okay. I don't want her telling my family I'm missing."

"You'll put her in immediate danger," Keira said.

"We've got your cover under control," Sandra said, walking back to her computer screen. "I found two unclaimed corpses that will work."

"Corpses?" I asked, numbness creeping over my body. "Corpses that will work for what?"

"Your death," Keira said. "Anyone who is called into this life has to have their death faked. It's the easiest way to—"

"Fake my death?" I wobbled a bit and grasped the back of a chair to steady myself. "I can't... die."

"We already switched out your DNA with that of the female corpse," Sandra said.

I shook my head, trying to digest all the new information. "How did you get my DNA?"

"You used one of those genetic testing kits you send through the mail," Jiong said. "It was easy to hack into their system and swap out your DNA results for that of the corpse. When they test her DNA, it will match the one the genetic testing company has on file for you."

My mother, I thought. She had given us all DNA tests for Christmas the previous year. She was curious to know if Miller and I took more after her or Dad. As expected, the results came back that Miller and Mom shared more traits, while Dad and I were practically the same person. Not that we needed DNA tests to know that.

"Your dental records and blood type were also switched out to match hers," Sandra said.

"The official story," Jiong said, "is you took an Uber in the middle of the night to the store for some cough medicine. Feeling a bit under the weather is what your late-night text to your publicist said. There was a mechanical issue with the brakes. The driver missed a curve and ended up off the road, down a large hill, and into a ditch. You were thrown from the car when it rammed into a tree, and you died instantly. No suffering. The fake Uber driver also died."

"They haven't found the car yet," Sandra said. "It may be another day or more since we hid it in a heavily treed area."

Out of everything they said, I latched onto an inconsequential tidbit. "An Uber? But, I didn't hire an Uber."

"We hacked your phone to make it look like you did hire one, and we already transferred the money out of your account last night," Jiong said. "According to your bank, it was paid to Uber. You were a pretty generous tipper, too."

"Oh," I said, still not fully grasping the more important parts of the conversation. "That's good to know. I do like to tip extra, especially to the friendlier, chatty drivers."

"Um, Mads," Keira said, "why don't we continue on the tour?"

"Sure," I said. "We'll let these two get back to faking my death with a random corpse. And, then maybe later, we can write my eulogy."

"Is she okay?" Sandra asked, though her question didn't deter the swirling of my thoughts.

"I wonder where my parents will bury the fake me," I said. The rambling in my brain exited through my mouth without concern for how others might view my temporary insanity.

"We never really had that conversation about my impending death, given that I'm only twenty-eight. I don't even know what *their* after-death wishes are. Maybe I should ask them next time we talk."

"Did you break her?" I heard Jiong ask, but I didn't react. My mind seemed to be, indeed, broken.

"I tried not to," Keira said, slipping her hand around my arm. "Mads, why don't we go back downstairs and let you rest for a bit?" Her tone rose slightly, as if speaking to a child.

Like the obedient non-prisoner I was, I followed her out the door and to the elevator. As we rode down to the main floor, Keira spoke quite a bit. Asked questions, made statements. Every word entered my ears, but failed to penetrate anything else. Even as we exited the elevator and I paced behind a couch in the lobby area, I didn't pay her much mind. All I could think about was my family learning of my death. Would my dad's heart hold out? It had only been three years since his second heart attack. Another one could—

"...Xanax," Keira said, bringing me out of my thoughts. I had stopped pacing at some point during her spiel, and she stood in front of me.

"Excuse me?"

"I took a lot of Xanax when I first got here. Helped me through those first few weeks. Definitely helped when I learned about my fake death. I still take some from time-to-time. It's the only thing that will get me to sleep after some of our outings."

I stepped back a few paces. "Your death was faked, too?"

She chuckled. "Those who are born into this life have it so much easier than ones like us. They aren't on the grid to begin with, so they get to keep every bit of their lives. Ones like us... well, we have to disappear from society to keep our loved ones safe."

For the first time since that morning, what she said made me realize that she was trying to *help* me. That she had truly been in my position in the past, and she wanted to get me through everything I had to face.

"Why did you stay here?" I asked. "Why did you agree to them faking your death?"

"For the same reason none of us called into this world ever leave it. There's so much you still have to learn, but when you do, you'll want to stay, too."

My gaze dropped to the white-tiled floor as I considered her words. All of them. Everything she had said since we first met last night under extraordinary circumstances. Even Mr. Smith's voice reverberated through my mind. The things he had hinted about, things he didn't say. The further I spiraled down the black hole of the unknown, the more surreal the world became.

"Xanax would be great tonight," I said.

"I'll add it to the menu."

I walked around to one of the couches to rest for a moment. Looking up at Keira, I watched her take apart her ponytail and redo it. The simple act brought me back to reality. I'd always had a tendency to ramble about nothing when stress consumed my veins. I must have appeared to the others to be a complete mess, possibly unhinged. Most likely insane.

Yet, despite everything, something inside of me remained calm. As if learning about my impending, public death didn't matter. It was almost expected, and I had no understanding as to why.

"Keira," I said. I slouched over, my palms resting on my knees.

She sat on the couch catty-corner to me. A long moment passed as we stared at each other, comfortably seated in silence, as if we'd known each other a lifetime.

Her lips curled up on the left side, her kind eyes dropping a tad, as if determining what to say.

I beat her to it. "I'm sorry I'm such a jerk."

Her eyes widened with an audible gasp, and she touched the back of my hand. "You're not a jerk. You're actually handling this better than I did." A chuckle rolled across her lips. "At least, so far."

Her smile relaxed me. "I don't know what it is," I said. "I

should be freaked out right now. I should be yelling and screaming for my release. But, something is telling me I'm safe here, in this complex, with you and Garrett. Even with Mr. Smith."

"You *are* safe in here. Out there, it's much harder to survive, but these walls afford us so much protection."

"Why? Why am I not freaking out?"

"It's the mark." Her hand reached for the back of her neck. "There's something about it that instills calmness inside of us. It makes us know where we belong. Who we belong with." She raised her hands on either side of her and glanced at our surroundings. "This is home, for all of us. These people are our family."

Like warm fingers caressing my neck, the mark made itself known for the first time that day. It seemed like its own entity. Alive. As if it shot dopamine direct into my system, my anxiety faded, and a fog floated through my brain. The strange high forced my lips into a smile, and I relaxed into the couch cushions.

"It's the best feeling, isn't it?" Keira asked. "The mark gives us the ability to handle situations that would drive others over the brink. But, we need it, with all that we deal with."

"What *do* we deal with?"

"I know there's a lot to learn still, but let's take it slow today. You don't have all the time in the world, like I did. I learned everything over a few months' time, but I'm a night stalker. There are lots of us. There's only one chronicler for each complex. Makes your job just a bit more important and gives you less time to ease into this, but you can at least take today to rest and get used to being here."

"Sounds like my luck," I said, only half-joking.

"You know, when I first came here, my life was a mess. Parents divorced and constantly battling, even though us kids were all adults. Didn't really speak to my siblings. My sister spent more time in jail than out, and my brother was a scam artist turned motivational speaker who had changed his last name and made up a different family background for his traveling act. I worked nights at a truck stop diner, telling myself every tip I earned was savings for college, even though I was barely making rent." She laughed. "But, at least the diner served awesome milkshakes."

"Never underestimate the power of a chocolate milkshake," I said, and we both broke into brief laughter.

"How *did* you get here?" I asked when the chuckling ceased.

"My journey was a lot easier than yours. Garrett's mom showed up at the diner one day, told me the itching in the back of my head wasn't only in my mind. Something about her... It was easy to leave my old life behind. Nothing chasing us or anything like what you went through."

I noted her word choice of "nothing" versus "nobody." Author's habit. Always dissecting words used around me, searching out that hidden meaning.

"Faking my death didn't mean much to me," she said, "but I understand how hard it would be for those with family who cares."

My parents would be devastated at news of my death, especially Dad. I could only imagine how Liz would react. My books in progress would go... unfinished. Every artist's nightmare, having an incomplete work. I should have run for the nearest door. How could I trust that my life was even in danger, that something was after me? Everything at the hotel could have been staged, and these people were experiencing a mass delusion.

Yet, the mark on the back of my neck was real. Something was happening in this place, *to me*, and I had overwhelming, instinctual knowledge that Keira was right. That as soon as I found out what exactly this place was and discovered my part in it, I wouldn't want to leave.

"I know you said to take it slow today," I said, "but I want to know more."

"Are you sure? We can take as much time today you need to—"

"No," I said, hopping up from the couch. "I need to know. I need to understand."

"Okay," she said, rising from the couch. "Let's go to the fourth floor."

Chapter Nine

The humming started as soon as the elevator doors opened to the fourth floor.

At first, I thought my ears deceived me, but slowly, the humming increased in intensity despite the volume remaining soft. It tugged on something deep inside me – my soul, possibly. The strong magnet pulled me down the tiled hallway with no furnishings on the walls until Keira and I stood in front of an ornate wooden door. I ran my fingertips over the carvings, various symbols, and letters I didn't recognize, despite them seeming familiar.

"What is this place?" I asked with no intentions of receiving an answer.

"Can you read them?" Keira asked from beside me.

I jerked my head to look at her. "I don't even know what they are. How could I read them?"

"You'll be able to decipher them soon enough, along with all the old languages."

"Old languages?"

"Latin, Greek, Hebrew, Enochian. I'm sure I'm missing a few there."

"Hieroglyphics?" I asked in a joking tone.

She snapped her fingers. "Yup, that, too."

I let out a laugh at the insanity of it all. "I barely passed Spanish my first year of high school. Foreign languages are not my thing, let alone strange symbols and things like Latin. I mean, I don't even know what Enochian is."

"An occult language that John Dee and Edward Kelley brought into play back in the 1500s. Some believe it's the lost language of angels because that's what Dee and Kelley said, but in 1832, The Order discovered that…" She waved her hand and smiled. "You know what, not important right now. You'll learn all this soon enough."

"And, let me guess. It will all start making sense."

"Okay, maybe I say that a little too much, but it's true." She reached into her front left jean pocket and pulled out an iron key with some of the same symbols from the door on it. "This key opens this door. It's your key and yours alone. This is the only copy, so you need to guard it. No one – not from this complex or from another one or anyone else – is to have this key, even if they ask for it."

She held it out to me to take, but I hesitated. "Why do you have it then?"

"We all have our roles here. One of mine is acting as Keeper of the Key during any… transitional periods between chroniclers. But, now that you're here, it's yours. Not even I can ask for it back."

I stared at her for a moment before asking, "Is there always a chronicler here at the complex?"

"Yes, other than the times that a new one is called up."

Dread knotted my stomach, but I asked the question anyway. "What happened to the last chronicler?"

A shadow crossed her eyes, and she averted her gaze. "Our… lifestyle… well, it doesn't really guarantee us long lives."

"She died?"

"He," Keira said. "He died ten days ago."

"I'm sorry," I said. A heavy silence lingered in the air for a long moment, clouded over by her revelation of my predecessor's fate.

My thoughts punched me in the gut. *Predecessor*. Less than twenty-four hours since I met Mr. Smith and I was already so far down the road of accepting the situation, just as Keira had predicted. Whatever this place was, whatever a chronicler did, I didn't see any way I could just walk out. Not knowing someone died.

I snatched the key from her outstretched hand before logic had its way with me and I changed my mind. *No turning back*, I thought as I pushed the key into the hole above the doorknob. The lock clanked as it unlatched, and the door creaked open on its own accord. Stale, pent-up air blustered through the cracks and shoved itself down my throat until it rested in the deepest crevices of my lungs.

A shift – both audible and physical – racked my bones, while the hum melded with my mind. Symbiotic energy whistled through the air, flowing from my body to whatever was in the room and back again. This place... I *knew* this place. It knew *me*.

And, though I didn't understand why, nothing in the world could tear me away from it now.

I shoved open the door and stepped over the threshold. The hum embraced me and encouraged me to wander deeper into the darkened room, but I turned instead to look at Keira. She remained in the hallway, watching me.

"Aren't you coming?" I asked.

She shook her head. "That's your domain in there. No one else goes in but you. Well, except for Spencer."

Of course, he has access, I thought. "What's in the room?"

"A few thousand years of chronicles." She grinned and peeked around me as if she were a child sneaking a glance into a forbidden room. "Every bit of this complex's history is in there, along with everything you'll need to know to help us accomplish our missions."

"Ahhhh," I said, finally getting it. "Chronicler. My job is to keep a record of everything the night stalkers do."

"Along with helping us with research. There's so much information contained in there, but you can sift through it like no one else. As a chronicler, you're plugged into it because of your mark."

"The humming," I said.

She leaned over, and in a confidential tone asked, "It started? I hear it's the coolest experience to hear the chronicles communicating with you."

"Is that what it is?" I chuckled at her excitement. "It's a little overwhelming right now. Not sure how to process it yet."

"From what I understand, it will become second nature for you. It dims down when you're not near the room, and you'll be able to ignore it when you need to."

I turned back around and stared down the short hallway leading to a dark room. "What do I do when I'm in there? Where do I start?"

"It will come to you," Keira said, "just like everything else."

Though her footsteps retreated from me, I didn't glance back or say "goodbye." My mind focused on the room and the humming that wrapped itself around me in a comforting embrace. Even if I thought the events at my hotel were staged, I couldn't argue with the mark or the hum. If everyone in the complex was brainwashed into believing, then I was now counted among them.

Several steps forward, and I closed the door behind me, shutting myself inside the dark room. I palmed the key and pushed it down into the front pocket of my jeans. Another two steps and fluorescent lights flickered on overhead, revealing the contents of the room: books.

I moved into the inner sanctum of the room and rotated a few times. Thousands of books littered the shelving on the walls, not just on my floor, but two floors above me. The three spiral staircases climbing to the next levels made me smile. It was as if the room had been built around the antique fixtures. Along the walls, ancient sconces lit the way, and I imagined chroniclers of old using dim candlelight to read the volumes of information. I could almost *see* them seated at carved desks as they recorded even more volumes, most likely with feathered pens.

The thoughts filled me with wonder beyond anything else

I'd experienced.

I was home.

Not knowing what came next, I lowered my eyelids and inhaled the centuries of history. The humming silenced itself, and I instantly missed the sound. I moistened my lips and let two words roll out in a whisper.

"Blood seekers."

The humming startled my eyes open, and a smile crossed my face. I followed the crescendo of the hum to a bookshelf in the back of an annex. My fingers tickled the spines of books until the hum reached the highest of pitches. I pulled the book off the shelf and examined the worn leather binding. *"Conquisitor Sanguinis et Mortis."*

My mind translated the Latin with no effort: "Seekers of Blood and Death."

"Oh… I can read it." My hushed statement filled the air around me, and I took the book back to one of the wooden desks. Time for me to learn all about those things Mr. Smith had said were chasing me in my suite. I brushed dust off the front cover and cracked it open.

Chapter Ten

After hours of sitting in the wooden chair, poring over every chronicle that spoke to me and fascinated by the marvels of the texts, I came to one conclusion: These people weren't crazy.

They were absolutely, completely, and most definitely certifiable.

If half – only *half* –the things I'd read about were true, why the hell would any of them ever want to get out of bed in the morning? Let alone, rush into battle with creatures and otherworldly monsters that could slash and maim and eat and bludgeon and do all kinds of horrible things to night stalkers *before* killing them?

Yet, I knew everything in the chronicles to be true. All the paranormal happenings – my mark, the humming, reading a foreign language, my insanely calm nature at the situation – reinforced that knowledge in me. My fear should have consumed me in that moment, but the mark kept me levelheaded. It reminded me that *because* the chronicles were true, something had to be done about it.

That was where the night stalkers came in. To stop the horrid things creeping around in shadows. To save the innocents out there who had no idea such things existed. And, to protect future generations from as many of those things as possible. My job was to document it all, to ensure that future chroniclers and night stalkers had all the information they needed to perform their duties and not get themselves killed. Hopefully.

I stretched my hands over my head, then in front of me. My neck cracked as it rotated. Closing the book on the desk, the fourth one I had read in a row, I stared at the cover. Older than the rest, the foreign language on the front translated in front of my eyes, just like the rest of the words in each book. Like a pixelated puzzle revealing itself, the letters would appear in their original language, then unscramble until I saw the English version. My brain became faster at deciphering the more I read, but the concept still overwhelmed my limited, human capacities of logic and reason.

The door to the library opened, startling me out of my chair. Keira had said no one could enter there except for me. And, Mr. Smith.

My head shook and mouth scowled as he entered the main part of the library, but I didn't speak.

He walked over to the desk, grabbed the book I was reading, and looked at the cover. Without comment, he tossed it back on the desk. "Keira wants to know if you're ready to eat."

Having deprived myself of food all day, a soft groan erupted from my stomach.

"She says you haven't eaten anything today," he said. "You have to keep your strength up at all times. You never know when we'll have to leave, and I can't have you lagging behind because you're on a diet, or whatever."

The man clearly had no idea how to speak to anyone, especially women. "I'm not on a diet," I said, seething as I rose from my chair. "And, I'll eat when I'm damned good and ready." Another growl filled the space between us, and I grasped my stomach as warmth crawled across my cheeks. "I just so happen to be ready now," I said a little quieter, trying to save a little bit of dignity.

Picking up the book, I whirled around and re-shelved it. When I returned to the table, Mr. Smith waited for me. He started for the door without a word, but then whipped around halfway there. "Just so you know," he said, his finger up in the air, "I'm not happy about you being here."

"Really? I thought you were this welcoming with everyone. Always showing off your lovely disposition."

He grunted.

"So, what is it about me? Is it because I'm a woman? Are you threatened by—"

"You've been here for just over twelve hours. You don't know what you're talking about, and with the reckless behavior you demonstrated last night, you're likely to get someone killed. You have no business trying to be a chronicler."

"If I understood correctly, the mark chose me, so there's nothing for me to 'try.'" I clasped my hands together. "Oh, I get it. The last chronicler was your boyfriend, and now you're taking your loss out on me."

Darkness crossed in front of his eyes and cinched his features – and I wanted to take back everything I had said. I opened my mouth to apologize, but he stopped me.

"He was my brother." He left the room, leaving me drowning in regret.

Damn your mouth, I thought, my heart breaking for not only him, but the others in the complex who lost a friend and colleague. I had gone way too far. The man had lost his brother just over a week earlier, and I was the replacement. I realized it wouldn't have mattered who had been next in line for the job; Mr. Smith would be just as angry, and he had every right to that rage.

I don't know how long I sat in that stiff, uncomfortable chair before Keira's voice called down the hall. The thought of staying in the library forever crossed my mind, since no one else could enter, but then I remembered they could just send Mr. Smith back in to retrieve me. Then again, maybe I could have stayed there until I died, and then he would happily retrieve my rotting corpse, just so I wasn't around to speak another cruel word to him. There would be a new chronicler, they would get along great, and I'd be in a much better place.

My rumbling stomach won out over my internal protests, and I sulked down the hall and out the door. I didn't say a word to Keira as I locked up the library and pocketed the key.

"Are you okay?" she asked.

I started down the hallway with her, toward the elevator. "I did something really stupid."

"Given that Spence came back up all sour, I'd say you two had it out again."

"No, it's my fault." I halted and waited for her to turn around. "He riled me up again, and I let him get to me, and I said the dumbest thing about the last chronicler, and then he told me it was his brother, and I think I should just go back home now, even if one of those blood seekers finds me and kills me, and—"

She stepped toward me and rested her hand on my shoulder. "Oh, honey, stop. Whatever transpired, it's okay. Look, Spence has been really screwed up since his brother died. He'll be screwed up for a long while. Anyone would. He's not really hostile toward you, he just doesn't know how to express his anger at losing his brother."

"And, I'm the one taking his brother's place, so I make the easiest target."

"Unfortunately, and I'm going to talk to him about it."

"No," I said. "Please don't. I would feel horrible about that, worse than I already do. I don't know how I'm going to face him now."

"It's not fair to you, someone who just entered the complex and is still learning about everything. You've been thrust into an impossible situation, and he's making it worse."

"It's really not his fault, either." I let out a loud sigh and crossed my arms. "Where is he now?"

"He went to his room. Didn't say anything to me about what happened."

"Where's his room?"

"It's the one to the right of yours."

I smiled at Keira, grateful to still have a friend in all this. "I'm going to apologize. I don't know if he'll accept it or cuss me out, but I can't let it stay like this."

"He won't cuss you out," she said. "He's not like that. Not the real Spencer."

I pulled in a deep breath and nodded. "I hope you're right."

Chapter Eleven

I must have paced in front of Mr. Smith's closed door for twenty minutes without knocking. At one point, I retreated to my room and sat on my bed, wishing I could disappear. Nothing I could do would take away what I had said to him. Despite being in anger and as a direct result of his insults, I had no excuse.

My knuckles rapped against the white wood, and I waited for a response. None came, not that I expected it to with my light taps. I knocked again, louder this time. I couldn't keep putting off talking to the man.

The door swung open, and I came face-to-face with Mr. Smith. He didn't say a word, only crossed his arms and arched his brow.

"I, uh..." I took a deep breath and dug deep for the courage to speak. "I wanted to apologize. I was out of line. I didn't know—"

"No," he said. "You didn't know."

I bit my tongue at his snide remark and continued with my apology. "You're right, and I shouldn't have said anything when I didn't know. Even if it wasn't your brother, it was someone you worked with. You've all suffered a loss, and now I'm here, which can't be easy." I paused, but he didn't say anything. "I guess... I don't know." I looked down and tried to find the words. "I guess I'd like to start over with you. If that's still possible."

A long moment passed without a response. I raised my gaze to his face and, for the first time, saw the turmoil behind his eyes. The dark shadows under them, the creases around them that probably appeared after losing his brother. This was someone who had never spoken about his grief. Someone whose pain rubbed so raw, he didn't know what to do with all the overwhelming emotions. All the anger.

"I suppose I wasn't the best person to bring you here," he said. "Even though that's my job, I should have passed it on to someone more qualified... under the circumstances."

My heart ached at his attempt at an apology. I opened my mouth to say more, but my name sounded from inside his room. I peeked around him and saw a television on with a familiar voice coming from it.

"Is that... Is that my dad?" I asked.

Mr. Smith stepped aside. I brushed past him into his room and faced the television mounted on the wall. Not only my dad, but Mom, Miller, Holly, and Liz all stood around a podium with New York City police officers next to them.

My hand flew over my mouth as I spied the tears in my dad's eyes. Every wrinkle stood out on his face and rapid aging consumed his neck. My mom had forsaken her contacts for an old pair of tortoise-shell-rimmed glasses that magnified her reddened eyes. Miller held his head down with his arms around both Mom and Holly, and Holly's hands circled under her pregnant belly. Liz held her hand on Holly's shoulder.

"If anyone knows anything about our girl, please call," my dad said, the quiver in his voice wrenching my heart. "Magpie, if you can hear me... Well, just know we love you."

"I love you too, Daddy," I whispered.

An officer walked up to the podium – Lieutenant Manuel Graves according to the writing at the bottom of the screen – and said something about police efforts to find me, but I tuned him out. Mr. Smith's presence beside me caught my attention.

"Why didn't you tell me this was on?" I asked.

"I didn't know about it when I saw you in the library. Jiong called to tell me a few minutes ago." He used a remote to switch off the television. "Things like this, though. Makes it harder to leave that life behind."

I had spent most of the day in the library, gobbling up as much information as I could, not once thinking about my family. How could I have done that? Forgotten about them while they toiled and agonized over my disappearance.

"I need to call my dad," I said. "They need to know I'm okay."

"That isn't a good idea," Mr. Smith said.

"Keira said the same thing, but there has to be a way to get in touch with them. If I can just explain what's..." The thought stuck in my throat. What could I say that wouldn't sound insane? That out of billions of people, some mark selected me to be part of a centuries-old secret order that fought creatures to keep the world safe? That those creatures came for me, and I needed them to not say anything to anyone or the creatures might target them to get to me? That disappearing from their lives was safer than sticking around?

"Brent and I wanted to join the circus."

The odd statement made me glance at Mr. Smith.

"When we were kids, I mean."

I nodded, realizing Brent must have been his brother's name.

"We saw a circus on television once and thought it would be the best way to be free of this place. See the world. Have no responsibilities." A wistful smile found his lips and lingered there. "Brent wanted to be like the Flying Graysons, even though he was the clumsiest person."

"The who?"

"Oh, um, it's from Batman. Before Robin became Robin – the original Robin, that is – he was Dick Grayson. As a kid, he was an acrobat with his parents. That's what Brent wanted to do."

I watched his eyes darken once more as mourning for his brother sullied his expression. Now that I knew what plagued him, I wanted to take back so many of the things I'd said to him in the past day. He had lost his brother to this life; I was also in the process of losing all my loved ones. If only I'd known, somehow, about his plight, maybe we could have found common ground sooner.

"The problem is, Madison, that once you learn what's out there, you can't walk away from the mark or the calling. You can't run away and join the circus. There's no more living in that world, with all the innocent, naïve people who don't even know there are monsters to believe in."

Sadness burned through my soul, threatening to dismantle me. In the library earlier, I had thought blood seekers were the worst thing I'd have to face. But, even after losing my family and friends, my career, my *life*, there was the possibility of growing close to my new family and losing one of them. Or, dying myself. Keira had said living in this world usually meant an early checkout from it.

"You're right," I said. "Leaving isn't an option. Not after the things I read about blood seekers."

"And, there's much more than blood seekers out there."

A tremor ran through my body. Blood seekers were bad enough, but other creatures? I didn't want to ask about those, though, not at that moment. I still had to repair my relationship with Mr. Smith. "I didn't mean what I said earlier in the library."

"I did," he said.

I stepped back, thinking we had made progress. That we had connected.

"It's nothing personal, Madison, but I just lost my brother. This world that we live in doesn't stop for death. It doesn't allow us time to mourn or even bury our dead."

"You can't bury your own brother?"

"He fell on a mission, and his body had to be left behind."

Every word Mr. Smith spoke explained more of his attitude, his brashness. Even my family would bury me, despite it not being my corpse. How could he ever get closure if he couldn't bury Brent?

"I wasn't there when he died," he said, "and I should have

been. My job is to protect the chronicler, and I couldn't save him. Another mission came up at the same time, and I had to be there while he had to go on his. It was the first time we went on missions without each other."

Yet another layer to the mystery of Mr. Smith unraveled. Something else snapped into place in my mind. "Is that why you had to come get me even though you just lost him? Because it's your job?"

He nodded. "After our first two meetings, I knew you wouldn't call me when the burning started. I followed you to dinner, then to your new hotel. Waited for you to fall asleep until I broke in, which wasn't hard since you left the balcony door unlocked."

Though I chided myself for leaving it open, I realized the mistake saved my life by allowing him to get into the suite without trouble.

"Anyway," he said, "I wouldn't be happy with anyone who came in to replace Brent as the new chronicler, no matter who it was."

"I'm not here to replace him," I said, stepping forward. "I may be the new chronicler, but I'm not ever going to try to replace him. What happened was horrible, and I do not want to take away from your pain or loss. But, I have a job to do, same as you. I didn't ask for this mark, but now that it's here, I have to answer the call. I just hope my presence here doesn't upset you too much or render you unable to do your job."

"I can do my job just fine. I won't let another chronicler die."

Each clipped word tore through me, cueing me to close out the conversation. *Don't take it personally*, I thought. That was what he had told me, and I needed to remember that every time I dealt with him. "Will you keep me updated on my disappearance? I'd really like to watch any future press conferences."

"It's easier not to know."

"I have to," I said, though I wasn't sure I could handle watching my family suffer again. "Just until I know they've buried the fake me and they can start moving on."

"So long as it doesn't interfere with *your* job."

I deserve that. "I won't let it interfere."

"Are you going up to eat dinner now?"

My rumbling stomach had long since stopped. "I think I'll just go to bed." Before he could protest, I added, "I'll be sure to eat a full breakfast in the morning to make up for it. I just need some time alone tonight."

He seemed satisfied with the explanation. "I'll see you tomorrow then."

Without another word, I left his room and retreated to my own. After kicking off my shoes, I hopped into bed and pulled my familiar blanket over me, grateful for the small reminder of home.

Chapter Twelve

Knocking on my door roused me from a deep sleep filled with dreams of blood seekers overrunning a book signing. I wondered if Keira's Xanax cure would take away future nightmares.

Glancing at the clock, I noticed I had only slept for a couple hours. I slipped out of bed at the second set of knocks and opened the door. Keira greeted me with a food tray consisting of a sandwich, chips, and water. Before I could thank her, she whispered, "I'm so sorry."

My forehead creased as I let her in. "What are you sor—"

Garrett barreled into my room. "Mads! How are you?"

I almost laughed at his childlike glee. Apparently, Keira had passed my nickname on to him, which didn't bother me. "Hey, Garrett," I said.

"Brought you a late dinner," Keira said. "It's not much, but I figured I couldn't go wrong with a turkey and swiss sandwich."

"Perfect," I said, my stomach reminding me I had neglected it all day. "I really appreciate it."

"I also put a little something extra on there," she said, winking.

I looked at the tray and saw a small medicine cup containing one pill. Xanax. I winked back at her; our little secret anxiety medicine club.

"Do you mind if I join you?" Garrett asked. "My dinner is just outside."

"He wants to pick your brain about your books," Keira said, rolling her eyes. "I tried to tell him to leave you alone for a couple days, but—"

"No, no!" I said. "It would do me some good to talk about something other than the complex or blood seekers or my family."

"I told you," Garrett said to Keira under his breath.

I laughed at the way the couple fit together. Garrett seemed to be a child in a grown body, with Keira constantly reigning him in. All the while, love ruled them. It shone in their eyes as they stared at each other and penetrated their playful tones of voice. The perfect relationship.

"All right, then," Keira said, smiling. She raised the tray. "I'll take this out here so you guys can talk books."

I followed them into the lobby area where Garrett's dinner waited. Keira set the tray down next to his plate of food and unloaded it.

"I'll leave you two bookish kids alone," Keira said, tucking the empty tray under her arm. Turning to me, she said, "If he becomes too much—"

"It's fine, really," I said. "Like I said, it will do me some good. And, now that I won't be able to finish my books for the mass public, maybe I'll keep writing them just for Garrett to read."

His eyes lit up and his mouth dropped, all while keeping his large, toothy smile. "Really? You mean, I'll be the only one to read any future Madison Shaw novels? I can't believe it."

"Just so long as you don't go all *Misery* on me and torture me to write them the way you want," I said.

"I wouldn't dream of it!"

"But," I said, thinking my situation through, "I guess that means I can write more books the way *I* want to. You know, when I'm not doing chronicle stuff."

"There's always an upside," Keira said. "You two have fun." She wandered toward the elevators, carrying the empty tray.

After Garrett and I sat on the couches, I tore into my sandwich. The turkey, cheese, mayo, lettuce… all of it basic, but my taste buds interpreted it as the best damn turkey sandwich in the history of sandwiches.

"I have so many questions for you," Garrett said, a mouthful of his sandwich wedged in his cheek. "This is like a dream come true, for me at least. I couldn't believe it when they said you were the new chronicler."

I swallowed some water and chuckled. "If only everyone here felt the same as you. But, trust me. I'm nothing special."

"Ah, just ignore Spence," he said. "He's still dealing with Brent, his brother."

"Yeah, he told me."

"He did?" His face scrunched up, and he averted his gaze. "Huh."

"What?"

"Oh, nothing. He's just usually pretty closed off, even with me." His expression cleared, and he picked up his sandwich. "On to better topics. I love what you did with *Withered Flowers*. I mean, you lead the reader down this path where we think everything is roses and sunshine, but we didn't know the secrets Heath had. Suddenly, everything got destroyed to the point that there was no coming back, no matter how you wrote it."

I smiled at the thought of the ending. "I was nervous writing that, but I didn't see the story any other way. The characters could never end up together. They weren't meant to be."

"Well, I loved it. It was so *real*. It wasn't a happy ending just to have one."

"I wish my critics and ninety-eight percent of my readers agreed with you."

"Yeah, they just didn't get it. It was brilliant the way you wove the story together. So many twists that I never saw coming. Even when I re-read it, some of those things still get me."

"Wow," I said. "If we weren't in this life, I would hire you as my publicist, at least for that book."

Redness crept into his cheeks, but he played it off. "Nah, your publicist does a great job. What's her name? Elizabeth... something?"

"Liz Pohl," I said. "She is great." Heaviness weighed my heart down, pushing it into my stomach. "She's my best friend, too. I miss her so much."

"How long have you known her?"

"Going on three years now. She makes this whole bestselling author thing so much easier. I couldn't do it without her."

"She hasn't been with you since the beginning of your career? How did you guys meet?"

"At a coffeehouse in San Diego, believe it or not. There was some roadwork going on in front of my house, and the noise was too distracting to write. I went to a coffeehouse around the corner from me to work. It was packed with nowhere to sit. She was sitting alone, saw me with my laptop bag, and invited me over. We haven't been apart for more than a day ever since. Until this, of course."

"Sounds like a great friend."

"It's gonna be hard to navigate the world without her," I said, "but I know what we do here is so important. Too important to walk away. Besides, Keira is amazing. She's really helped me transition."

He beamed with talk of his wife. "That's Keira. Since she wasn't born into this life, it took her a long time to adjust, but my mom helped her out a lot. She likes to pass that on to anyone new, not that we get new ones that often."

"Speaking of which, I'm sorry about Brent. I can't imagine what it's like to lose family like that."

"This is a dangerous world," he said. "I don't think any of us expect to live to see fifty. But, it is hard to lose someone so young."

"How old was he?"

"He had just turned twenty-six. Five years younger than

Spence."

My eyes closed at the new information. I couldn't imagine how hard it was to have to say goodbye to a sibling, but at that age, it made it so much worse. Then again, in my world, people often lived past ninety. Spencer and Garrett were raised with the knowledge that death could come at half that age, if not sooner.

I realized that I thought of Mr. Smith as Spencer for the first time. It could have been the intimate nature of our earlier discussion, or maybe I was growing accustomed to his unusual personality. I wondered if he had always been abrasive, or if it was the life that made him that way, each loss causing him to sink deeper into a pit of darkness and death. Maybe a little of both.

"You'll get used to everything," Garrett said, interrupting my thoughts. "Everyone here is gonna love you. Not that we don't miss Brent, but we know we can't hold that against you. Spence knows that, too, even if it's harder for him."

"It's okay," I said. "He's going through a lot. Everyone is. And, then I come into the picture and disrupt the complex. I don't blame him." I laughed and leaned forward. "Although, he really doesn't like romance writers, does he?"

Garrett's hearty chuckle filled the room. "He never understood why I read romance novels. Always made fun of me when we were younger."

"You have to admit, it is a bit unusual."

"I know, but maybe I wanted something happy in this world of monsters. Something to look forward to when I became an adult. And, you'll never hear Keira complain about my romantic side, even if she doesn't have a soft bone in her body."

Even in the short amount of time I knew them, I could see her taking the more masculine role in their relationship. "So, tell me something," I said. "Do you watch *90 Day Fiancé*?"

He gasped, and his eyes grew. "Are you kidding? Every chance I get!"

"Sounds like we're gonna be television buddies," I said, a

laugh in my voice.

"I would say so," he said. "Okay, now, tell me what book you're working on now."

Happy to have forged such a strong connection with not just Keira, but also Garrett, I smiled and launched into a spoiler-free synopsis for my new book.

Chapter Thirteen

The next morning arrived much too early. A headache pounded my brain awake, most likely from eating so little the day before. Possibly from the late-night discussion about books and reality television shows with Garrett.

After showering and dressing, I headed out to the lobby. I glanced at Mr. Smith's closed door. I considered knocking to see if he was awake, but decided against it. No need to stir the beast.

I entered the elevators and pressed the button for the second floor, remembering Keira had said that was the location of the kitchen. The hours she gave me for meals eluded me, but she also said the kitchen was always open since many in the complex couldn't make it during the normal meal times.

When I found the kitchen, several people were seated at tables in a cafeteria-style room. A buffet was set up near the back of the room, with a soda dispenser and coffeepots next to it. Shyness overcame me when I noticed every eye trained on me, the new girl on her first day at a new school. I held my head down and shuffled my feet over to the table where Keira and Garrett sat.

"Morning, Mads," Keira said. "Did you sleep well?"

"Actually, yeah," I said, sitting down. "The bed is very comfortable."

"I wasn't sure if you would ever get to sleep or not," she

said, "since my husband decided to bombard you with questions for half the night."

I laughed, as Garrett groaned. "We had a great discussion," I said. "Turns out we like all the same authors and television shows."

"Thank goodness," she said. "I am so tired of him trying to make me watch that reality television crap with him."

"It's not crap, babe," he said. "You're gonna offend Mads."

"Oh, no," I said. "It really is crap, Garrett. But, it's a guilty pleasure, so it gets a pass."

"Are you gonna eat?" Keira asked.

I glanced around the room. "I, uh…" I lowered my voice. "I think I'm a little buffet shy this morning. Everyone keeps looking at me."

"Oh, I'm sorry. I forgot you haven't met the others yet." She jumped to her feet and cleared her throat loud enough to stop all conversation. "Hey, everyone. I want you to meet Mads. She's the new chronicler, as you may have guessed."

Crimson spread from my cheeks into my neck and down into the rest of my body. I must have looked like a lobster with the all-over blush. It was hard enough to do a book signing and reading in front of people who enjoyed my writing and wanted to meet me. How many of my new colleagues were going to be like Mr. Smith, thinking I was trying to replace Brent?

"I thought your name was Madison," one of the men said at a table two over from us.

"It is," I said, "but everyone calls me Mads."

"Cool nickname," another man said.

"Do you all want to go around and tell her your names and what you do?" Keira asked.

It really is the first day of school, I thought. *Is there a pop quiz later?*

The round robin of introductions began with the table to our left. It would take a few days – maybe weeks – to learn everyone's names and roles, but I did my best to remember them all. I didn't want to be *that* girl, the one who couldn't place faces or names, even though I was terrible with both.

The man who questioned my nickname was Harvey Pratt, another night stalker. His hardened face, unruly beard, height, and mass – a possible bouncer or leader of a motorcycle gang in a former life? – made him appear scarier than Mr. Smith, but his smile gave away a softer side. He welcomed me to the group and let me know he would help me adjust in any way he could.

I made it a point to remember Jia Chen, the Information Coordinator for our complex. I recognized the sibling resemblance between her and Jiong before Keira informed me they were twins. Jia said we would work closely together as new information came in from either night stalker missions or from other complexes. I would need that information for not only my chronicles, but for her to share with others like us around the world.

The nurse with slicked-back, over-gelled hair for the complex was also present at breakfast. He introduced himself as Antonio Aleo and gave me the location of their clinic on the eighth floor. He said Doctor Chandra Porter had left earlier that morning for a medicine and supply run, but that I should stop by the clinic later so I could meet her.

When the maintenance man, Jim Higgins, finished his introduction, the chef, Diego Costa, came out of the kitchen to meet me.

Once everyone had spoken, I thanked them all for the warm welcome. After they resumed their personal conversations and eating breakfast, I turned to Keira. "Where are the other night stalkers? Are there five more?"

"Yes," she said. "Spence, Garrett, Harvey, and myself plus five more. They're on a scouting mission. We were tipped off a couple nights ago on the location of the nest of blood seekers who killed Brent."

"Really?" I asked, not sure why the surprise in my question. I should have assumed that priority number one of the complex was to eliminate the blood seekers responsible for killing him. "They moved from their last location?"

"They vacated as soon as our team retreated," Garrett

said. "It was a brutal defeat for us, and we weren't ready for their numbers."

"The others are doing recon now so that we don't end up in the same position," Keira said.

"Is there anything I need to do?" I asked, eager to assist.

"Learn as much as you can about blood seekers," Keira said.

"We will leave in a week to wipe them out," Garrett said.

"I'm going with you guys, aren't I?" Nerves trembled inside of me, despite knowing I would eventually end up on a mission with them. After I had one under my belt, I hoped they would grow easier, but the fear of death became real in that moment.

"We need you, Mads," Keira said. "But, we'll have the whole team this time, and Spencer will keep you safe. He won't let anything happen to you. Not after Brent."

Something about knowing Mr. Smith would watch over me made me feel safe. "What exactly is my role on these missions?"

"You're our information girl," Garrett said. "We rely on you for last-minute info. But, more than that, you record everything that happens for the other complexes and for future chroniclers."

"Information is what drives us forward in our quest to eradicate all blood seekers," Keira said. "One day, we will get there. Maybe not in this lifetime—"

"You don't know that," Garrett said. "It's possible that we could—"

"I'm more of a realist," Keira said to me. "As if you didn't already know that."

I smiled at them. "I think some hope is good. What's the point of all this if you don't believe the fight will be over one day?"

"Exactly," Garrett said. "And, I want kids. Lots and lots of—"

"Then, you better hope men can start giving birth soon," Keira said, laughing. "I mean, one or two, fine. But, lots and lots is out of the question."

Garrett jabbed his thumb in her direction. "She wants to be a night stalker until the end of time, I think."

"You can't do that with kids?" I asked.

"I could," Keira said. "Most women end up giving up the life once kids come into the picture, except for maybe the occasional run. Too dangerous, and even though the others here would help raise them if something happened to us, no one wants to leave their kids without a parent."

The risks of my new life continued to show themselves, something I would have to get used to, and soon. Miller and Holly crossed my mind. Their biggest concerns were getting kids to preschool and playdates. Whether to put them in public or private school, or to home-school them. If they should get them involved in sports at a young age or wait for the children to make up their minds if they wanted to play sports. For Garrett and Keira, the decision to have kids would alter their lives beyond anything parents outside the complex could imagine.

Garrett's hand shot up and waved to someone across the cafeteria. I twisted my neck in time to see Mr. Smith enter the room wearing a plain gray T-shirt and black shorts. He paused and caught my gaze for a tense moment before walking toward us. When he reached us, I realized his eyes weren't as hard and weary as they were the last time we spoke.

"Hey, Spence," Keira said. "Join us for breakfast."

"I was heading up to the gym," he said. "I just wanted to stop in and see how Madison is."

I flinched. Did he say he was interested in my well-being? "I'm good," I said. "Thank you. How are you?" My stilted questions reflected my stunned mind.

"Well, thank you." He shifted his weight. "After breakfast, how about we meet up in the library? I'm sure you have questions about blood seekers that you need answered prior to our next mission."

"I, uh... Yes, I do."

"Great," he said. "I'm going to work out and eat. I'll meet

you up there in a few hours."

"Okay," I said, barely getting the word out before he walked away.

He stopped to greet a few others in the cafeteria and disappeared out the door.

I turned back around to my tablemates. Garrett plowed through cheesy scrambled eggs, while Keira grinned in my direction. "What?" I asked her, wary of her strange smile.

She shook her head, but the grin remained. "Nothing, I'm just glad to see you and Spence getting along."

"Um, me, too," I said, rising from my chair. "I'm gonna grab something to eat."

"Yeah," she said. "Go help yourself."

"The bacon is cooked perfectly," Garrett said with a mouthful of egg.

I made my way to the buffet table, praying my time with Mr. Smith in the library would go smoothly, but also dreading the upcoming mission. My first, from which some of us might not return.

Chapter Fourteen

My right leg jittered, my foot tapping against the tile floor beneath me as I waited for Mr. Smith to make his appearance in the Chronicle Library. I had picked up the same book I started the night before, but something had changed from then. No humming. Not a peep from the books, the ones that sang to me and pulled me to them yesterday.

Not knowing what I did wrong, why I could no longer hear the chronicles, I rose from the desk and walked into the center of the room. I closed my eyes, even held out my hands. I focused with all my might, concentrating on the years of history around me. All those chroniclers before me that had sacrificed so much for the words on these pages. Had sacrificed themselves.

Still, nothing.

I don't know how long I stood like that, wrinkles around my squeezed-shut eyes, my lips turned down, a headache from all the concentrating pounding against my skull. I just needed some connection. Even if it were a small one, a slight sound… which I sometimes thought I heard, only to discover my mind was humming, not the books.

Had I lost my gift? Maybe, I was no longer chosen.

"You're trying too hard."

I jumped back at Mr. Smith's voice, losing my balance and crashing to the floor. My hands tried to cushion my fall, but they did little to stop the hard tiles from colliding with my backside at full force.

He laughed, a sound I had yet to hear and one I thought he'd never emit. I had barely witnessed a crack of a smile when he spoke of his brother, but to laugh at *this*? At *me*? Right *now*?

Many alternative, not-so-nice names for him ran through my mind alongside vile insults biting at my tongue for release, but I held them all back. The fall might have been a humorous sight, and I might have even laughed at myself, yet something about him laughing first… I wanted to murder him and hide his body in a dark corner of a library annex, never to be found as his rotting flesh melded with ancient, leather-bound books.

His hand floated in the air above me, waiting for me to reach for it. Despite his initial reaction to my fall, he still demonstrated a small spark of humanity.

Unfortunately, his chivalrous act came much too late.

I ignored his hand and pushed myself up from the floor. Dusting off the back of my jeans, my anger rose as his laugh echoed in my ears.

"For the record," he said, "I tried to help."

"After you laughed at me. I didn't realize it was so funny to watch someone fall." I rubbed my lower back, the telltale soreness of a bruise already starting. "I probably broke my tailbone."

"You didn't break anything," he said.

"Well, it sure as hell hurts like I did." My skin prickled like the rising of fur on an enraged cat, and my anger released with dramatic flair. "I could have died! My head could have hit—"

"Hit what? You're a good three feet away from the bookshelves, and the wall is much further away than that."

Stubbornness swelled in my mouth, contaminating my words. "But, still. You don't know what could have happened." My index finger accused him of ill-will. "It's your fault, too. You shouldn't sneak up on people like that."

"I didn't sneak up on you," he said. "I was several feet away from you when I addressed you."

His logic annoyed me far more than anything else he'd said

since we first met. "Yeah, well, then you could see I was deep in thought trying to—"

"Connect with the chronicles?" He paused for a moment, but I didn't respond. "I saw you, and you were doing it wrong, so I stopped you."

I crossed my arms and shifted my weight. "I've been here one day. How am I supposed to know what's right or wrong when telepathically communing with books?"

"That's what I'm here to teach you. Part of my job. Guiding you and protecting you."

"Maybe I don't need your guidance and protection then."

An amused smile parted his lips. "Okay. I guess you were just about ready to have a breakthrough when I barged in and made you fall. And, since you have no questions about blood seekers or chroniclers or night stalkers, I'll just go on about my day." He swiveled on the balls of his feet and headed back toward the door.

"I didn't say…" I clamped my mouth shut when he stopped walking and rotated to face me.

"What?"

My only hope at understanding what I read in the chronicles stood in front of me, packaged up as Mr. Smith. I forced my pride down to the pit of my stomach and shoved it into the growing tumor of bitterness toward him. "I might need a little guidance. Just to get started, though. After that I should be—"

"I get it," he said. "You're a quick learner. I'll be equally quick about my guidance."

His sarcasm didn't miss its target, but I let it slide. He seemed to have taken lessons in snide at the same college I did. Excelled, really. But, he was up against a master, and I would strike back. When I could think of something to say.

"Your problem is you're trying too hard," he said. "You need to relax. Don't try to force the chronicles to communicate with you."

"I don't even know how to communicate with them in the first place."

"Last night, you were reading about thirteenth century blood seekers. How did you find that book?"

"I don't kn..." I stopped when I realized I *did* know. "I closed my eyes and said the words. 'Blood seekers.'"

He watched me for a moment without speaking, compelling me to explain further.

"I didn't know what to do when I got in here, so I just said it. Was that wrong?"

His voice lowered, and he shook his head. "I haven't seen a chronicler do that so quickly. I thought you might have picked up a random book."

A compliment? Or, perhaps, he didn't believe I could possibly be *that* good to get it right on my first try. I glanced behind me, wondering if anyone knew exactly how many books resided on the shelves. It looked like thousands... tens – if not hundreds – of thousands. "It might be a little hard to pick a random book and hope it's the right one."

A corner of his mouth lifted in a half-smile. "Someone could get lucky, I suppose."

"If I were that lucky..." I stopped before I could finish the sentence. With the recent loss of his brother, it seemed Mr. Smith had much worse luck than me. "So, how do I do that again? The books don't seem to be... talking to me today. I thought maybe I'd lost my place here."

"Once the mark chooses you, that's it," he said. "No going back, no way to lose your place. We simply have to train you right."

As much as I bristled at the idea of spending more time with Mr. Smith, my inability to connect to the chronicles was more frustrating than he could dream of being. It left a void in me, as if a vital organ had jumped out of my body in the middle of the night. I didn't just want to hear the hum of the chronicles; I needed it to survive.

"Show me."

He chuckled again, and I stepped back at the foreign sound. "It's not as easy as showing you. Besides, I can't connect with them like you. I can only guide you."

"Then, guide me."

He inched toward me as he spoke, the volume of his voice dropping to a mesmerizing level. "You need to relax. You won't be able to let the chronicles in if you don't relax. Drown out everything around you."

I sucked in the air around me and exhaled, wiggling my arms before letting them fall against me. My back muscles let go, but my legs remained stiff to hold me up.

"You're gonna fall again if you're not careful," he said. "Don't relax your body. Relax your *mind*. The mind is all that matters in this room." His hands grasped my upper arms with a light touch, and his gaze locked onto mine. "Take a deep breath."

I followed his instructions, despite my overwhelming sense of vulnerability.

"Just focus on me. There's nothing else around you."

Falling under the hypnotic trap of his voice, losing myself in the well of his soulful eyes, I did as he said. My arms trembled under the weight of his hands, and I feared every emotion swelling inside me. Especially the ones I couldn't define – or didn't want to define.

"Now, close your eyes."

My lids tried to shut, but they fluttered open. A confession escaped my lips. "I'm scared."

If he could look deeper into my eyes, he did so in that moment, connecting us in a way I never wanted to experience. "There's nothing to fear. This is where you belong. This is what you were always meant to do. It will come naturally."

His words provided me the courage I needed. My eyes closed, and I let go of everything else except his touch. As much as I wanted to, I couldn't ignore *that*.

"What do you want to know, Madison?"

I heard Mr. Smith's question, but it was underscored by a low hum. *The chronicles.* I stemmed my growing excitement, afraid I might chase the sound away again. What did I want to know? "What are blood seekers?"

My question floated around me, through the air, into

oblivion, and I was rewarded with the hum. I opened my eyes and broke away from Mr. Smith. Vaguely aware of his footsteps behind me, I followed the sound until I ended up in front of another bookcase, one I hadn't seen the night before. Withering, light-colored leather covered the book calling to me, and though I snatched it off the shelf, once in my hands, I revered it. This book had spoken to me – out of all the books in the library. It held the answers I sought, even if I didn't know I needed them.

Mr. Smith's hand on my back jerked me out of my daze. "You did it," he said, his eyes and tone expressing surprise. "It takes others so much longer. Several days, at least, to even hear the call of the books."

"You said it yourself," I said, my confidence rising. "I belong here."

"You do. More than I realized." He removed his hand from my back and looked down. "I really need to apologize to you."

"No, you don't." I managed a smile, my first for him. "Just quit being such a jerk."

"Maybe." He shoved his hands in his jean pockets. Shrugging and looking past me at the bookshelves, he said, "I'll leave you alone with your books now. You have a lot to catch up on."

After Mr. Smith left, I stared down at the chronicle in my hands, which still hummed in a low tone as if eager to get started. "Yes, I do."

Chapter Fifteen

Much like the day before, I closed the book in front of me, my mind reeling from everything I had read about blood seekers. Based on the number of books surrounding me, my learning might never cease, and I feared overlooking vital information that could save someone while out on a mission.

Throughout the day, I discovered I not only could read several languages, but I had developed an ability to speed read. I had always envied those who could read at extreme speeds, but now *I* could do it, too. The rate at which I took in words increased with every page I turned, and yet I remembered every syllable. Two more superpowers, like communing with the chronicles.

I was going to *love* my new job. Just maybe not the part about blood seeker battles and flying heads. I definitely still dreaded my first mission.

Everything else came naturally, as if I knew how to do it all even before I was born. While in the Chronicle Library, time slipped by me, food could not deter me, and I had no thoughts of the family I had left behind.

But, blood seekers… they loomed over my surroundings as if in the room with me, hovering, waiting to strike. The more I learned, the more my fear of them consumed me. Even reminding myself that Mr. Smith and the other night stalkers would protect me did nothing to ease my anxiety. After all,

Brent had died with the same protections, minus Mr. Smith.

I wanted to know what went wrong. Know how to avoid falling victim to blood seekers as Brent had. Could I even ask that? The thought of his body still out there, somewhere, quite possibly devoured by blood seekers until he was unrecognizable and now in the throes of decay… it was too much for anyone to digest, let alone me, the one designated to follow through this insane maze, an underground world filled with monsters and hunters.

Out of everything I had read, I realized not one book had given me the origin of the blood seekers. I knew they fed on human blood, they resided in nests, night stalkers existed to kill them, and the best method of disposing of them was beheading. Beyond that, I had no information on *what* exactly they were. How they came into existence. Why they existed.

I closed my eyes and summoned the chronicles, which immediately responded in the now-familiar humming. I followed the sound to the second floor of the library until it led me to the book that would provide me answers. The barely blemished cover and English for the title caught my attention. I opened the book and read the date: 1964. The newest chronicle I had read so far had been penned in 1786. My curiosity piqued at what differences there might be in the almost two-century timespan between the books.

Back at my desk, I flipped through the pages, noticing that the chronicler who penned the book, William Davies, had inserted his own beautiful renderings of battle scenes between night stalkers and blood seekers. I prayed that I wasn't expected to illustrate my chronicles, given that my ability to draw anything better than a stick figure would be a much more surprising superpower than reading foreign languages.

When I reached the correct spot in the book, a full section on the origin of blood seekers, I rested my head in my palms and dove into the text.

We encountered a small nest of blood seekers on our travels yesterday. Though slight in numbers, their strength was formidable. One of our night stalkers, Lucille Averill, fell during the battle, but ultimately, we destroyed the nest.

It is noted that very few chronicles to date explain the nature of blood seekers. Rather than writing down their origins, we have kept it strictly as oral tradition for thousands of years. I shall attempt to relay the legend here, for the future of our kind is dependent upon understanding both our past and our enemies.

The creatures date back to the time of the Egyptian curses upon the Pharaoh Ramses II and his land. God sent great punishments to fall upon those who would not allow the Israelites safe passage out of Egypt and continued to enslave God's people.

Upon release of the fifth plague, that of diseased livestock, God allowed the Devil to open the gates of hell, if only for a moment. A demon unlike any other escaped and feasted upon the livestock. It carried within it a virus unknown to man. The virus spread to the livestock, causing great calamity and disease.

Unaware of the demon's curse, the Egyptians consumed the meat of the infected livestock, passing the virus to man. Eventually, the virus was partially responsible for the death of all Egyptian firstborn, who had taken part in eating the largest portions of the diseased animals. Night stalkers soon rose up from the Israelites with the sole purpose of destroying the blood seekers and stopping their reign upon God's earth.

The blood seeker infection appears to begin in the lymphatic system, spreading throughout the organs and causing death. Yet, something in the virus keeps the mind alive. As the rest of the body decays, the blood seeker ingests the blood of humans to slow the process. Should they fail to drink blood, they shall die, however, we cannot count on this as a means to their destruction.

Beheading is the best-known method of killing a blood seeker, though we continue our search for other ways. We have yet to be successful in eradicating the demons, and other creatures have risen from the depths of hell for us to battle, delaying our studies of blood seekers.

The opening of the Chronicle Library door jarred me out of the tale, and I watched the hall for Mr. Smith to appear. When he did, I recognized a bit of disappointment in the wrinkles on his forehead and shadowing his eyes.

"Good afternoon," I said, hoping to ease any tension before it began.

"You mean evening," he said, stopping short of the table where I sat. "Keira said you hadn't been up for lunch or dinner."

"Evening?" My eyes darted around the room, as if it would give me some clue as to the time. "I didn't realize that—"

"That's the problem," he said. "You have to regulate yourself, Madison. The chronicles are amazing, but they will consume you if you're not careful. They can suck you in to the point that you lose track of reality. It's why I get on you about eating. Many chroniclers before you stayed more than a day in here, not stopping to eat or sleep. Let the books guide you, but don't let them control you."

Remembering his admonition from the night before about remaining well-nourished, shame colored my cheeks at once again having deviated from the norm of the complex. "I'm sorry. I didn't know so much time had passed. I don't have a watch, and there are no clocks in here."

"I'll make sure you have a watch with an alarm in the morning. I'll try to remember to come check on you more frequently as well. Are you ready to eat something?"

"I am, but I have some questions first. If you don't mind, that is."

He pulled out a chair diagonal from me and sat, arranging his seat so he faced me. "What do you want to know?"

"I just read about the origin of the blood seekers and night stalkers, but the chronicles mention other monsters out there."

"The Order has managed to keep monsters a secret for thousands of years. We can't let others know of their existence or the world would be chaos. Blood seekers are always our biggest threat, but you will come across much more in your life here. Right now, however, we are facing an influx of blood seekers, and there is a specific nest of them we are after."

"The ones that killed your brother."

"The same ones who were after you in New York."

I flinched. I didn't realize that the blood seekers chasing

me had also killed his brother. However, his appearance in New York made much more sense. "You're out for revenge, then?"

He hesitated, tilting his head as if weighing his answer. "All of us in the complex would like to see justice for what was done to Brent, but it's more than that. This nest has a powerful leader in place, so it and him must be destroyed before he can recruit more blood seekers. They're in our region, so they're our problem. It's why we went after them to begin with."

I hesitated with my next questions, not wanting to bring up bad memories. Instead of speaking, I looked past him, at nothing in particular.

"You can ask anything you want."

Permission granted, I glanced back at him. "What happened to Brent?"

"I wasn't there, so I don't know the whole story," he said. "The nest had divided in two sections, and we had to hit them both hard and at the same time so they couldn't warn the others. Our team was mostly successful. Only two escaped from us. The team with Brent... Well, that didn't go as planned. There were more blood seekers than our earlier recon specified. Brent somehow got separated from the others. He was cornered and ambushed."

"Did anyone else get injured?"

"No," he said, resting his clasped hands on the table. "We were very lucky in that regard."

"How many blood seekers were left?"

Looking down at his hands, he shook his head. "Half a dozen? Three dozen? There's no way to tell for sure. Since the recon didn't identify all the blood seekers, we don't know how large the nest was to begin with, and there may have been other offshoots from the group we weren't aware of. We believe many of them were hunting during our recon, which is why we miscalculated the threat." His eyes caught mine with a hard stare. "That won't happen again."

I believed him. Mr. Smith was not one to speak lightly.

"What else do you have for me?" he asked.

I closed the chronicle in front of me and asked, "How does ingesting blood keep them alive?"

He flicked the spine of the book. "We're still not completely sure how that works. We would love to capture a live blood seeker to figure it out, but that's not likely."

"Why not?"

"When night stalkers have tried in the past, the blood seeker just sacrifices itself. It's like a spy consuming a cyanide capsule rather than being forced to talk, but much more gruesome. I've watched a cornered blood seeker decapitate itself rather than be caught."

A chill rustled goosebumps on my arms, and the hair rose on my neck. "That's insane. Why… How? That's not possible… is it?"

"It rushed another night stalker, who held out his machete in defense. The blood seeker didn't hesitate to let the blade take its head." Mr. Smith leaned back in his chair, crossing his arms.

An unbidden movie played in my mind of the blood seeker purposefully running into a machete, but I shut it down before my imagination got too carried away. I didn't want to see anyone decapitated, but for one to do it to himself… I couldn't comprehend the motive. "Why would it do that?" I asked Mr. Smith.

"We think blood seekers communicate telepathically somehow. The way they move so seamlessly in nests, then they meet in random locations without any advance communication. It's like they're all connected. Our guess is that if one is caught, it would know what other blood seekers were up to. Interrogating a blood seeker could end very badly for the nest."

"Telepathy seems… I know that all of this is half-crazy given that I have books talking to me, but how would that telepathy work?"

"It might be some kind of pheromone carried in the virus, but that's the best we can surmise without further studies."

"A pheromone in a virus." I laughed. "I'll admit, I'm not the smartest when it comes to science, but is that even possible?"

"You have to remember, Madison, this is a complex, supernatural, demonic virus we're talking about. Science is limited to so-called reality. Even though blood seekers are very real, scientists across the world don't know that, so they couldn't possibly study them to find out."

I mulled over the theory. There was only one way to prove what they assumed. "You need a live blood seeker."

"It's the number one priority for The Order."

I caught the hesitation in his voice. "Just not for you."

"I want the blood seekers that killed my brother. After that, I'll follow along with whatever The Order wants."

"They don't approve of you going after this nest, do they?"

"They aren't exactly the revenge-seeking type. Revenge leads to mistakes, or something like that. But, I don't care. They can do whatever they want to me *after* those monsters are no longer on this Earth."

His distaste for The Order was not lost on me, and my imagination ran circles around the question of why. Had they done something to him, his family? Did he witness a higher up in a nefarious act? Discovered a conspiracy that ran through the darkest crevices of this secret society? Or, did he buck at the first sign of authority?

Probably the latter, I thought. Mr. Smith didn't seem too keen on the idea of being told what to do, even if it was the right thing. My speculations, however, were best left for a later time since the nest of blood seekers were at the top of his mind.

"I read that decapitation is the best way to kill them, but that was several decades ago," I said. "Are there any other ways to kill them?"

"We've tried lots of things, but decapitation is still the most effective. Several years back, we burned out a whole nest of them, but some of them survived. If the head is still attached, it's a possibility they'll survive. I don't like leaving things to chance."

I remembered the falling head that had terrified me the

night he rescued me. "The ones in my hotel suite before we went down the fire escape. Did you decapitate them, too?"

"Oh, heads definitely rolled," he said.

"I'd hate to be the one who discovered that mess." A thought crossed my mind. "Wait… Decapitated bodies in my room. You'd think that would be all over the news."

"I'm sure others in their ranks cleaned it up before anyone discovered them. Blood seekers don't like to leave behind evidence of their existence if they can help it."

"But, that still would have been a bloody scene, one that would have been difficult to clean. That would have made the news."

"Authorities probably kept out of the media since they're still looking for you. The police don't always report everything, especially if there's a bloodbath in a missing famous author's hotel suite."

For once, something about the situation of my disappearance satisfied me. "I'm glad. My parents would have freaked if they heard that." Sadness crossed my heart at the thought of my family. Again, I had gone almost the full day without thinking about them or their plight. "Have they… Have the police found my 'body' yet?"

"Not yet," he said. "I imagine it won't be too much longer."

"I don't know how others leave everything behind like this. I'm really struggling with it. It's got to be easier being raised in the life, having family who don't have to go through your faked death."

He smirked. "Yet, those like me who were raised in a complex would disagree. I would have loved to experience the world out there before committing to this life."

I could see his point. The grass was always greener, or so they said. "Do you have other family besides Garrett and Keira?"

"Garrett's dad, my uncle, is still around. He is high up in The Order. I believe he's seated sixteenth on the council."

"That's it? Your parents?" I regretted the questions as

soon as they left my mouth. How many times did they need to tell me that the life expectancy around here was very low before I finally processed it? "I'm sorry. I shouldn't have asked about that."

"It's okay. Dad died on a mission about ten years ago. Mom wasn't too much longer after that."

"They were both night stalkers?"

"Yeah," he said. "Hard thing about this life is that since we're pretty well isolated from the outside world and no one else can know about what we do here, everyone ends up marrying someone else in the life. Families end up being small and are often separated due to being called to serve at a different complex. Death can come early and quickly. Not many fifty-year anniversary celebrations in this place. Not many fiftieth birthdays, either."

Maybe growing up in the life wasn't as easy as I had believed. Being raised to know that everyone they loved could die young, knowing there wasn't much time to cherish anyone they cared about. Then again, every moment counted, so much more than in the world from which I came. Taking each other for granted, wasting time over petty things… they were probably foreign concepts to those in the complex.

"That can't be easy," I said. "And, I'm sorry about your parents."

"The only good thing about it is that they died before Brent. It would have destroyed them to lose him."

"I didn't mean to bring it all back up," I said.

"It's okay. You have questions, and I'm sure you'll have more. I'll be honest in my answers."

"Probably will have more questions as I sift through the rest of these books. But, I guess I need to know what I'm looking for. I mean, I'm learning a lot here, but there has to be something that's helpful for you and the rest of the night stalkers. Things you don't know, things that can assist in the mission to eradicate this nest."

"There are other components to your job," he said, "but until the other team returns from their recon, there's not much more for you to do but learn. You'll study not only blood seekers, but also other missions from the past. Learn what they did right, what they did wrong. When the recon team comes back, you'll review their reports and help us with whatever information we need to succeed."

"And, then I go on the mission with you. Sounds like an eighteen hour a day job I signed up for."

"Which is why we have to keep you well-nourished and in good shape. You ever go to the gym?"

"What's a gym?" Since learning I would join the night stalkers on missions, I'd had a feeling he would eventually force me to get into shape. I had never been the athletic type. Even watching sports seemed to wear me out.

"Got it," he said. "Let's go join the others for some dinner. Tomorrow morning, you're hitting the gym. Gotta get those muscles working again."

I groaned, but rose from my chair when he did. Grabbing the book off the table, I said, "You'll turn me into mush. What good will I be then?"

"We'll have you in peak physical condition in no time," he said, following me to the bookshelf so I could restock the book. "Can you at least run?"

"If there are cake and sweets at stake, then yes."

He laughed. "I guess I'll have to put something tasty for you at the end of the track as incentive."

"There's a track, too? You really do hate me, don't you?"

"It's not just you," he said. "It's all romance authors in general."

I swatted his arm and started toward the library door. With him trailing me, my eyes grew wide, and I restrained a smile. Had I just flirted with the enemy? A playful hit on the arm... Even with the shift in our attitudes toward each other, this was *Mr. Smith*. What the hell was I thinking?

Clearly, I wasn't. As I locked up the Chronicle Library, I resolved to change that immediately.

Chapter Sixteen

The streets of New York City bustled with the busy people occupying that corner of the world. I had been there several times over the years, but had never seen such a sight. Residents in business wear powered through sidewalks partially blocked by groups of tourists searching for that perfect photo opportunity. Cabs honked in an endless stream of irritating music, while deafening conversation made it impossible to focus on what Liz had to say.

"...of Liber..."

I turned my ear toward her and leaned over, hoping to catch every bit of her statement. "Say that again," I said, trying to listen only to her voice.

"Let's go to the Statue of Liberty today," she said, standing up from the café table where we had enjoyed our morning coffee. She straightened out her pencil skirt and smart business jacket — two things she would never wear on our days off from the book tour. Especially if we decided to play tourist and sightsee.

"We've been there twice already," I said, also rising from my chair. "Last time, you told me that was more than enough."

"I want to go on the boat, Mads." She walked around the table from me and grasped my hands. "You promised we could go this time."

I shook my head at her insane statements. "But, you get seasick. The last time we were here, you took several Dramamine pills, and it still didn't help."

"I won't get sick this time. I promise." She tugged on my arm, and I followed her lead down the street.

Despite remembering the ferry in a different location, the ticket booth appeared just two blocks over from the café. The man behind the glass seemed to have stepped out of a carnival. Red and white shirt, straw hat, and a "step right up" smile on his face. A gold tooth gleamed from underneath his curled lips.

"Do I know you?" I asked.

"I don't believe we've met."

I unzipped my purse and pulled out my wallet, but he stopped me.

"We don't accept your money here. You're too important to have to pay."

"No, please," I said. "Let me pay." I slid two ten-dollar bills into the slot under the window. "There's two of us."

He made no move to take the money. "Like I said, you don't have to pay."

Without anyone having touched them, the bills disappeared from the slot, but it didn't seem strange to me. The man removed his straw hat, and long, fiery auburn hair tumbled down into the shape of a mullet.

"Are you sure we don't know each other?" I asked again.

"Eventually, we all know each other," he said.

Before I could ponder the strange statement, Liz yanked my arm again in the direction of the ferry. "We're going to be late!" She broke into a run, and I stumbled to keep up with her as we shoved our way through another crowd of tourists.

"Slow... down." The breathy words sounded as if I were having an asthma attack.

Liz didn't seem to hear me as she continued dragging me toward the ferry. I gasped for air, and my free hand gripped the side of my torso as cramping seized my insides. I couldn't remember the last time I'd run, or even exercised on purpose.

Our feet thumped so hard across the ramp leading onto the ferry that I worried about falling through the wood. We entered the cabin, and I looked around at the occupants already settled into seats. They all turned to stare at me. Not at Liz. Just me.

The red-mullet ticket seller grinned, his gold tooth gleaming in the sunlight pouring into the cabin. How did he get there so fast?

I whipped around to see the other tourists that were surely coming with us. People always packed these ferries to capacity. But, no one tromped across the ramp, and no one stood behind us, waiting to get inside. The boat engine roared to life, and an unseen captain steered us away from the dock. Away from safety.

Liz pushed past me and sauntered over to a man in the corner of the room. She held out her hand, as if introducing herself.

The man kept his gaze focused on me. Narrowed, shadowed eyes, dark waves of scraggly hair reaching for his shoulders, several days' scruff covering his rigid jaw.

My skin crawled with all kinds of warnings about the situation. I stepped back until I hit the ferry's door. Instinct spun me toward it, and I pushed, pulled, and tried to slide the door open. The door didn't budge, as if it were welded shut. I searched the perimeter of it for hinges to learn how it was supposed to open and found none.

I turned around to find Liz. She stood next to the strange man — Dark Man, I thought — engaged in intimate conversation. She used every one of her telltale flirting moves: shoulders squeezed together slightly to create more cleavage, her hands roaming in front of her to draw his eyes to her best features, and that cute giggle that men seemed to drool over. And, Dark Man fit everything she considered her "type."

But, he didn't appear interested in her... not like the others who flocked to her side. No, his gaze roamed past her to watch me. The way he studied me left me vulnerable, naked. I wanted to call out to Liz, to have her come back by my side and stand strong with me against any unknown threat, but she seemed to have forgotten all about me.

Bathroom, I thought. Hide in the bathroom. Liz didn't need me; she appeared perfectly at ease with the man. I remembered using the restroom the last time we were on this ferry. I rotated, looking for the bathrooms. It was in the back, right next to the...

There were no doors left in the ferry at all. The windows had also disappeared. How had I not noticed the lack of sunlight in the cabin? A few florescent bulbs overhead provided the only means to see the room, and what I saw made me want to squeeze my eyes shut and wish myself away.

All the occupants in the room now stood, all facing me. Even Liz had stopped gabbing with Dark Man.

"Madison," Dark Man said. "What's wrong, my pet?"

The word "pet" slinked around my mind and left trails of goosebumps on my arms. I wasn't anyone's anything, let alone "pet." But, the way he said it – endearing and sensual, yet possessive and threatening – screwed with my thoughts of who exactly Dark Man was.

"You don't have to worry about making an escape," he continued. "There is no way out of here. Not even when you wake up."

I'm... asleep? I thought. I couldn't be, though. Everything around me was much too real.

"Turn your thoughts to me." Dark Man captured my gaze with his. "We're connected. You must realize that. It's all in the blood, dear Madison."

No! my mind shouted. We couldn't be connected. Then again, why couldn't I stop staring into those shadowy eyes? How had he hypnotized me so effortlessly?

"Liz," I said, my voice rattling. "Come on, Liz. We have to go."

She didn't move, didn't attempt a response.

"Liz, let's go," I said.

"She's not leaving," Dark Man said. "Neither are you. This is your destiny."

I ran my hands through my hair, from the top of my head to the back, until both palms cradled my neck, near where my mark resided. I had a much different destiny than this man realized. "Good thing you're wrong about that," I said.

"Am I?" His confidence raised every last one of my doubts, bringing them to the surface, where I was sure he could see them. "Liz," he said, turning toward her. "Come here."

When she faced him, he cupped her chin and lifted it. His face lowered to hers, his lips taking control of her mouth. She allowed his domination. Tears stung my eyes, but helplessness swallowed me as I watched my friend bend under Dark Man's control.

He parted from her, but her eyes remained sealed, her mouth open, as if savoring the remnants of his kiss. He motioned to Mullet Man, who rose on command and moved toward them.

"Liz, if you will," Dark Man said. "Let me have your neck, please."

My eyes widened as I watched her take Dark Man's hands and bend over at the waist. Dark Man steadied her, while Mullet Man lifted a machete.

"No!" I cried out, but the sharp blade fell and severed her head from her body. Strands of her beautiful blonde hair trickled down to the floor, landing in blood.

Dark Man picked up her head, while the others in the room attacked the rest of her. Her tattered clothes flew in different directions. Teeth – so many teeth – gnashed her bare skin, flinging bits of it aside as the monsters reveled in her blood.

An endless stream of tears rushed down my face, onto my shirt. I did what I could to control my sobs, but they echoed through the room, mixing with the sound of the creatures destroying Liz's remains.

"Madison," Dark Man said, his quiet voice somehow reaching my ears over the noise. "Come to me, my pet."

My legs complied, and my feet shuffled forward, despite my willing them to stop. My neck pulsed with the phantom feel of a blade slicing through it. I did everything I could not to look at Liz's head, but I did anyway, taking in her closed eyes and perfect smile frozen in time, as if she died in a state of ecstasy.

When I reached him, I had all but given up. My best friend dead, I saw no escape from the monsters devouring her, and the man who ordered her death puppeteered my strings. My gaze lifted to meet his, and calm rushed over me. Something inside my mind still fought, but the rest of my body surrendered.

Dark Man lifted his blood-soaked fingers and placed them in his mouth. He let out a soft moan of satisfaction, lowered his hand, and raised them once more – again, covered in the blood of my friend. His fingers moved toward my mouth, and though a spark of humanity battled against it, my lips separated and accepted his gift. The warm, metallic taste of my best friend's lifeforce reaffirmed the taboo nature of the act and aroused every nerve ending in my body.

Amidst the groans and crunching of the others ripping Liz apart, I raised up on the tips of my toes and accepted Dark Man's kiss. The horrible sounds beside me, the memory of Liz's head falling, the taste of her blood on his lips, somehow all fueled my desire for him.

He pulled away, frustrating me, but something told me he wouldn't withhold from me for long. "Tell me, my pet." His bloodied fingers swept across my cheek, down to my lips, leaving goosebumps in their wake. "Tell me what you want. What you need."

A surreal smile accompanied my response. "More blood."

Chapter Seventeen

Beat down, out of breath, and ready to jump off the proverbial cliff, I slumped to the sparring mat in front of Keira, who had worked out with me for the past four hours. My right leg threatened to fall off, and my left leg succumbed to pins and needles as soon as it hit the mat. One of the muscles in my right forearm twitched and spasmed with such fervor that I thought it might burst through my skin. Muscles in my back – ones that I had never known existed – screamed at me to allow them to return to their eternal slumber.

"I'm done," I said between heavy breaths, not for the first time. "No more, no more. You win. Everyone wins but me."

She laughed and sat cross-legged in front of me. "You look like I felt after my first week here. Just worse."

I tilted my head and scrunched my face up, still trying to catch my breath. "I didn't do well in gym class, and I avoid all forms of strenuous exercise. Unless it somehow involves chocolate."

"Oh, don't get me started on chocolate. Mmmm..." She stared off into nothing, quite possibly dreaming of the same room built entirely of the delightful treat as me.

"I don't suppose later we can sneak into the kitchen and whip up some brownie batter."

"I love brownies," she said. "Covered in melting, vanilla bean ice cream."

"No, I don't want to bake them. I just want to eat the batter. A whole bowl of it."

"Oh, damn. What are you doing to me?" She fell over on her side, held her head up with the palm of her hand, and stretched her legs out. "I love brownie batter. But, chocolate cake batter is so much better."

The taste of cake batter coated my tongue, as if I'd just shoveled a spoonful of it into my mouth.

"No spoon, either," she said. "Just thrust the fingers in there and lick it all off one by one."

I smiled at the thought, but then her words reminded me of my dream of blood-soaked fingers, and my stomach churned. I had woken up disturbed enough by the nightmare. Try as I might to forget every moment of it, bits and pieces floated back to me when I least expected.

"Hey," Keira said, sitting back up. "You okay?"

"Yeah," I said, trying to reassure myself more than her. It didn't work. "No, I'm not okay. I had a horrible dream last night."

She shook her head. "Those nightmares creep up on you fast."

"Did you have them when you first got here?"

"I think it's impossible not to. I still get them, too. The things we fight out there… it's too much sometimes. You've been in that library over twelve hours a day for two days in a row, reading about horrific creatures. I'd worry about you if you *didn't* have nightmares."

Still, something about my nightmare seemed different than the ones she had talked about. "Were yours really graphic and detailed?"

She paused, and her normally cheerful expression sobered. "There was this one dream that I had right after Garrett and I got together. We weren't married yet, but we already knew we would be one day."

I interrupted with a random question. "How long have you been married?"

"Three years now, so this nightmare was about a year

before our wedding. I still remember every part of it today, though. I dreamt that I was a blood seeker, and I killed Garrett."

"Oh..." My fingers retreated to my mouth. It had been hard enough watching Liz die and... and the stuff with her blood that I didn't want to admit to or think about. But, Keira had dreamt about killing the love of her life. "That must have been awful."

"It still is," she said. "I never told him. I never told anyone until now."

I laid my hand on hers in a reassuring manner. "I won't say a word."

"Thanks, Mads. So, what was your dream about?"

I leaned back and said, "About the same thing. Just involved Liz instead of... you know, a boyfriend or a future husband."

The return of her infectious laughter was a welcome sound. "Yeah, of course. Would be weird if you dreamt about..." Her eyes widened, and she stuttered over her next words. "Well, about someone you know but... you weren't dating... yet, or... or maybe ever."

"What?" It was my turn to laugh. "I think the thoughts of chocolate are overwhelming you, which is easy enough when we're both starved for oxygen from all that working out."

"If you think I'm tough, wait until Spence gets hold of you."

I groaned and fell backward onto the mat. Staring at the ceiling, I said, "Why can't I just work out with you?"

"He's in charge of all the training in the complex."

"I think he thinks he's in charge of everything here." I lifted my head to look at her and rolled my eyes. "God help me."

"You'll get used to him."

"What if I don't want to get used to him?"

She smirked, as if she held back a secret. "I don't think you have a choice."

"Don't I?" I crunched my abdominal muscles to sit back

up. "There's always a choice. How does one get used to Mr. Smith anyway? Every time he speaks, I cringe inside. That stupid, arrogant smile of his, like he knows everything."

Keira let out a restrained laugh, but I ignored it to continue my verbal rampage.

"Superiority, that's what it is. He thinks he's better than me because I just got into this life and I wasn't born into it, like him. The constant criticism, too. I'm not doing this right, or I should do this different. He doesn't even stop to think about my circumstances or that maybe this thing doesn't come easy for everyone. I just want to... punch him. Really hard."

She cleared her throat. "I get all that, I do. But, there's one other thing he is, too. He's really stealthy."

"Stealth... what?" Then, it hit me. The presence behind me. How long had it been there? I glared at Keira. "Why didn't you shut me up?"

"Probably because no one could get a word in," Mr. Smith said, walking to the side of the mat. "Did you even take a breath?"

I stifled my anger, but didn't back down. "Oh, I took a breath. If you would like me to resume without taking one, I'll be more than glad to demonstrate."

"No, I think we all got the gist. It's because I said I didn't like romance novels, isn't it?"

I couldn't believe he would chalk everything up to something so immaterial. "Oh, Mr. Smith. You really do have a limited world view, don't you?"

"I could say the same thing about you," he said. "It's all subjective."

Though his words rang true, I wanted to throttle the man. My fists balled up beside me, and I encouraged my lungs to only take deep, cleansing breaths.

"Get to your feet," he said.

"What?"

He gestured for me to stand up. "Up, now."

"I think I'm good," I said.

"Gotta see what Keira's been teaching you."

"We've only done running and cardio," Keira said.

"And, my limbs are ready to fall off," I said. "I think I'd rather go to the library now, if I can manage to pick up a book."

Mr. Smith stood over me, arms folded. "Researching will come naturally to you. This won't. I need you in better condition for this upcoming mission."

Him somehow being always right forced me to rebel even more. "I have a choice, you know. There's *always* a choice, and I choose the library."

"Actually, you don't have a choice," he said, "seeing how I'm in charge of the complex."

My jaw dropped, and my head whipped around to look at Keira for confirmation.

She nodded to my unasked question, that amused smile lingering on her face. "He's the senior night stalker for our complex, so he runs the place."

"I think we'll add that to the list of things that you should have told me sooner," I told her. My aching muscles begged for mercy as I stood and faced Mr. Smith. "What elaborate torture do you have in mind for me today?"

"For starters, stand up straight and round your shoulders. You can't fight slumped over."

I followed his directions and lifted my balled-up fists to my chest.

"I'll get some pads," Keira said.

"No padding," Mr. Smith said. "She'll do better if she fears getting hit."

My eyes widened. "You'd really hit a girl?" I knew my words set women back several years, but didn't care. This was one arena where I didn't care for having "equal rights."

"As tempting as it is," he said, "I'll try to restrain myself. Hit me here." He patted next to his left shoulder. "As hard as you can."

Tightening my limp arm muscles, I lashed out my fist. It bounced off the meat to the right of his shoulder. Weakly. The impact jarred my wrist, and I shook out my hand.

Mr. Smith seemed unfazed. "Again."

After another limp punch, he directed me to try again with my left fist to his right shoulder, which ended up an even bigger failure.

"Aren't you supposed to be protecting me on these missions?" I asked. "Why do I need to do any of this?"

"Yeah, my job is to protect you, but if it gets chaotic and I lose track of you, I need you to be able to defend yourself."

"I have no strength left," I said. "This isn't doing an ounce of good."

"You'll get there," he said. "How are your reflexes?"

"What are those?" When he didn't smile at my joke, I said, "They're as nonexistent as my muscles."

His fist smashed into my right shoulder.

I jumped away from him just after the impact. "Ow!" I grabbed my shoulder and stepped back until I reached the edge of the mat.

"You're right," he said. "You have no reflexes at all. We'll work on that."

"You hit me!" I rubbed my sore skin. "I think you dislocated it."

His disbelieving eyes warned me he'd probably do it again if he could get away with it. "It's not dislocated."

I looked at Keira for some sort of intervention.

"He did restrain himself," she said.

I turned my anger toward Mr. Smith and repeated my argument. "Your job is to protect me. I shouldn't have to learn any of this."

"As I just told you, I will do my best to protect you, but if you can't run, you're going to be dead within minutes of walking into a blood seeker nest. If you can run but can't protect yourself, you might make it through one mission before you're food for them."

Keira grimaced. "Sorry, Mads. I have to go with Spence on this one. This isn't an easy job and training is a big part of it."

"We only have six days before the next mission," Mr. Smith said. "That's not a lot of time to get you in shape."

"Well, then maybe the mark should only choose people who can survive this life," I said. "I'm exhausted and overwhelmed and have been running and doing cardio for the past four hours. I just want to go back to the library."

He huffed out the air in his lungs and studied me for a moment. Moving toward me, he extended his hand and placed it on my upper arm. "I'll do everything I can to help you learn this. In a couple months, you'll be in the best shape of your life. But, until then, you need to work with me."

My guard dropped, and regret consumed all other emotions. I didn't understand why, but Mr. Smith pushed me to the brink of insanity every time I saw him. Yet, he was doing his job – protecting me by giving me tools I needed to survive. I also had to remind myself that he was not only driven by his life as a night stalker, but by needing revenge for his brother's death. I couldn't imagine what I would do if someone had murdered my brother, Miller. I'd probably be just as brash and focused as Mr. Smith.

"I'm sorry I give you such a hard time," I said just loud enough so he could hear. "I'll work with you however I need to."

"Thank you," he said, letting go of my arm. "Why don't you clean up and spend some time in the library? We can do this again before dinner, then let you rest up for the night."

I averted my gaze. His eyes peeled back too much of that rough exterior for me to look into them for long. I turned to Keira and thanked her for her help before leaving the gym.

Chapter Eighteen

The discolored, blemished pages from the journal of a fifteenth-century chronicler blurred the longer I stared at them. More than five hours into my study session and I had only made it through one book. What I really wanted to read eluded me, no matter how many times I spoke the words to the library: *Blood seekers in dreams*.

Despite Keira putting me at ease when she revealed she had also dreamt about blood seekers, as soon as I entered the library, something nagged at the back of my brain. Something that told me the dream had been *too* real. Yet, the chronicles seemingly held no answers.

They did lead me to something else, though. Something I had been wondering since learning about blood seekers. What did they look like? The ones who had broken into my hotel suite appeared normal in the darkness, but they were only silhouettes. One held a gun, so I knew they had hands. But, decaying from the inside out could not be attractive, if they even rotted on the outside. From what I had learned, the blood kept them from complete deterioration, but that *smell*. The odor of death. I couldn't imagine ever getting used to it.

I flipped the pages in the journal before me, seeking out what I knew had to be in there. I stopped about halfway through the book when I ran across it: a sketch of a blood seeker. I skimmed the few paragraphs above the drawing and learned it was a creature the chronicler had encountered and beheaded that very night. As if to prove his words, a light smear of blood graced the bottom of the page. I stared at it for a moment with my heart beating irregularly, contemplating that it belonged to a blood seeker who had been dead for centuries.

The first sketch on the blood-stained page was the profile of a normal man with nondescript features. Since drawn in pencil with various shades of black and the yellowed page acting as the contrasting white, I couldn't tell his color of eyes or hair. Both appeared to be dark from the heaviness of the lead in those sections. His nose, pointed sharply toward his thin lips, had a hump in the middle, lending to a crooked appearance, one that could have belonged to any face from that era.

On the opposite page, another sketch of the man, facing toward the reader, portrayed him with an open yet unsmiling mouth. His teeth all appeared to be in order, though slightly rotted in some areas, as indicated by shading. Circles underneath his eyes dragged his lids down to gaunt cheeks, and deep wrinkles penetrated his forehead. Still, nothing abnormal.

My breath shuddered in my throat at the next page. The chronicler had again drawn the same blood seeker, but the new picture showed him with his head tilted back. The missing lower jawbone gave full visibility to the roof of his mouth. There were several small slashes drawn in behind his normal teeth – three rows of them, each row with a smaller number of slits. In front of his teeth, there were three more. The chronicler had placed arrows pointing to the openings, with a note written in block letters and a double underline punctuating the words: "BLOOD TEETH."

The picture on the right page demonstrated what he meant. He had drawn the blood seeker at a different angle, but still without the lower jaw. Where the slashes had been, jagged, pointed teeth had filled in the spaces. Some grew at crooked angles, making the creature even more fearsome.

While the need for the teeth made sense, given their lust for blood to stem their own decay, I thought back to my dream and how the blood seekers had torn apart Liz's body. The teeth alone wouldn't have provided the capability for them to crush her into nothing while accessing her blood. The strength of their bite – possibly matching that of a crocodile – would have to be formidable to tear through bone.

But, I didn't know any of that before the dream. That the teeth in the pictures seemed to match those of the blood seekers in my dream terrified me even more. That damned dream.

After putting the book away and locking up the library, I headed to the elevator and rode up to the third floor. I wandered down the halls until I found Jia Chen's office, our Information Coordinator. Since she had contact with other complexes, she could possibly learn more about blood seekers and dreams for me.

Her back greeted me when I walked through the open office door. I second-guessed saying anything as she looked intent on whatever she wrote on the paper on her desk, but I needed to find some answers. My dreams were far too realistic to attribute them to my subconscious speaking out in the night, especially when it included details I had no way of knowing.

"Excuse me, Jia?" My timid, apologetic voice emerged just loud enough for her to swivel in her chair.

"Mads!" She jumped to her feet and rushed over to me. Embracing me in a hug, she said, "I'm glad you came for a visit."

I chuckled uneasily. I would eventually get used to all the warmth of the team, but I had never been a huggy-lovey person. Still, her arms reminded me that I wasn't alone in this.

After she released me, I returned her large smile. "I'm hoping you can help me out."

"That's what I'm here for," she said. "Did Keira or Spencer tell you what I do?"

"Just that you're the Information Coordinator, and you communicate with other complexes."

"That's me. Have you already gotten so far in the chronicles that you have info for another complex or The

Order?"

"No, nothing like that." I moved over to a second desk that formed an "L" shape with hers and leaned against it. "I actually have a question. Something that I can't seem to find in the chronicles here. Would anyone else be able to help?"

"Sure," she said, "depending on if they have information on it. Our chronicles have some reproductions of books from other libraries, but most of the books are different from library to library. They can easily contain information we don't have." She sat in her chair and picked up a pen and pad of paper from her desk. Poised to take notes, she asked, "What did you want to know?"

"I was curious about dreams and blood seekers."

She tilted her head and squinted her eyes. "Dreams?"

"Yeah, like are there any stories about blood seekers in dreams?"

"That's a new one for me," she said. "I've heard about people having dreams about blood seekers and other creatures, you know, as a result of all the work we do, but I have a feeling you're not talking about that."

Pausing, I considered my response. I hadn't been honest with Keira about my nightmare, even though the revelation about her own dreams eased my concerns a little. I had just met Jia officially, so it seemed odd to tell her first instead of Keira, but I had the feeling the people at the complex tended to share more than others in the outside world. I was never one to confide in others. Liz had been the only person I entrusted with my secrets, and now I couldn't consult her.

I opted for a vague explanation. "I had a weird dream last night about blood seekers," I said, "but Keira says she has them, too. It just freaked me out, that's all."

"Of course, it did. You've not seen one before, have you?"

"At my hotel two broke into my suite, but it was dark, so I couldn't see them. Mr. Smi..." I stopped myself, remembering only I called him that. "Uh, Spencer killed them before I got a good look. I did find some sketches in a journal, though."

She laid the pad of paper on her lap and leaned over in a conspiratorial manner. "Did you see the teeth? Those scare me the most. Thankfully, I've only seen a couple in real life. I'll take working in my office over being a night stalker any day."

I couldn't disagree. "How did you come to the complex? Or, were you and Jiong born into it?"

"Long family history in the life. My grandmother was a night stalker. I used to listen to her stories as a kid and pray that God never put me in that role. When our marks came in, both Jiong and I were called to be part of The Order, which is where most of our family is called. We've only had three night stalkers in our family over the generations."

"The Order – tell me again. Is that the main group that are neither night stalkers nor chroniclers?"

"Yup," she said. "Since my family has been part of this for so long, I knew a lot of people from other complexes, so it seemed natural for me to coordinate information. Plus, my dad is seated on the high council for The Order. It's a bit bureaucratic, but what isn't?"

My head spun with the new information, but her story fascinated me. "I have a lot of learning to do still. A lot of adjusting, too."

She waved her hand at me. "You'll get it. Chroniclers learn faster than anyone else. Kinda comes with the job."

Warmth overflowed in my heart at the kindness shown to me by others in the complex. Tears surfaced in my eyes, but I swallowed them back. I had never been a crier, despite many readers crying over my books, yet emotion overwhelmed me. Everything that had been absent in my life was now in place. I missed my family – my heart *ached* at the thought of them and Liz and what they must be going through with my disappearance. But, the people at the complex who had been strangers just days before… they were my true family. And, there was no other place I wanted to be. Just as Keira had said would happen, I never wanted to leave.

"I'll look into that dream thing for you," Jia said.

"I appreciate it."

"Oh, and just so you know," she said, "my office is also the place for gossip. I always hear it first. Comes with the job. If you want to add the flair of drama to your life or if you learn something scandalous, you know where to find me."

I laughed and nodded. There always seemed to be that one person who knew the scoop on everything – and everybody. I thought of a thousand questions to ask her, but needed to get back to the library before Mr. Smith herded me into the gym for another body-breaking workout.

We exchanged our goodbyes with another hug – maybe I was becoming a huggy person after all? – and I left her office, intending to return to the library until Mr. Smith dragged me out. But, when the elevator doors opened, Mr. Smith stood there, unmoving, waiting for me to join him.

I shrugged, but didn't enter the elevator, nor did he make a move to exit. My shoulders stiffened and back muscles tensed. Even though he had opened up to me about his brother and family, something about being near him roused the sarcastic beast inside of me. My instincts told me to always remain on defense around him. Throw more bricks at the wall between us. Seal them up tight with the strongest possible mortar. Don't just push him away, but shove as hard as I could and run in the opposite direction.

"Going up?" I asked, hoping he was heading downstairs and I could wait for a vacant elevator.

"No," he said, finally exiting the elevator. "Neither of us are."

I restrained a groan. "Is it already time for the gym?"

"No, not now. Maybe later, after dinner."

After dinner? Earlier, he had said we would hit the gym before dinner. He didn't strike me as a man who altered his plans on a whim. "What's going on?"

"The other team will be here in a few hours."

My eyebrows shot up. "The team doing recon on that blood seeker nest?"

"Yeah," he said. "We'll have a long night planning, I'm sure. But, there's something else."

The sudden softness of his voice caught my attention. His eyes held sadness... no, *sympathy*. My heart dropped into my stomach in anticipation of his next sentence.

"They found your body."

And, just like that, with four words whispered through the air, I had died.

Chapter Nineteen

There was something liberating about death. Morose, heartbreaking... moments filled with endless pits of melancholy, but liberating, nonetheless. I no longer feared my parents finding out that we would never reunite. They – and I – could start to heal.

A short-lived sentiment.

Standing in the computer room – Sandra and Jiong sitting behind their desks, Keira's heavy arm around my shoulders, Mr. Smith blended somewhere into the background – I could only stare at the largest monitor. I couldn't stop the New York City police lieutenant from speaking to the media, couldn't quench the pain of my family standing to the side of the podium, couldn't reach out to Liz, whom my mother leaned against, to let them know it was all a lie. I was alive. No need to worry. No need to cry.

Waves of guilt crashed into me, threatening to buckle my knees as tears streamed down my dad's face. Guilt for accepting my new role so easily, for thinking of those in the room with me – even Mr. Smith – as my destined family. For wanting to help others, to save them, from creatures like blood seekers and other nasty things I had yet to learn about. For not being more selfish by denying this life and returning to my blood, God-given family.

But, with that guilt, came the knowledge that my death had

freed me from the ties of the real world. I could embrace my duties as a chronicler and help save lives without the fear of my family or friends being in danger. One day, after my actual death, others would read my chronicles and hopefully learn from them, as I was learning now from the chroniclers before me. My life would offset the pain my family and friends suffered today, tomorrow, and in the future, and hopefully temper my guilt.

"Her identity was partially confirmed through dental records," the lieutenant said to the crowd. "Unfortunately, due to the accident, there were some teeth missing or chipped, so we could not obtain a one hundred percent match. We should have DNA confirmation in about a week, but despite this, we are confident the female body recovered is Madison Shaw."

"Does that mean her body isn't being released to the family yet?" a male reporter asked from the front row of press.

"Not until we have that definite DNA confirmation. The family has also requested an autopsy, although no foul play is suspected."

"When will there be a funeral?" the same reported asked.

The lieutenant cleared his throat. "It may be a couple weeks before a memorial service is held, but that information will come later and directly from the family."

"What about the other body?" An unseen female reported shouted the question.

"We do have the name of the Uber driver," the lieutenant said, "and believe it to be him, but we are waiting on confirmation. He had no immediate family, so we're searching for DNA and other records to assist with the identification. Who else?"

I shifted away from Keira's arm. "I think I'm gonna get back to the library."

Her scrunched-up, concerned expression elongated into a different apprehension, possibly mixed with a bit of shock. "Are you sure?"

"Yeah, I have a lot of research to catch up on and this…" I waved my hand toward the monitor. "It's just not something

I really want to hear."

"Okay," Keira said as I walked away.

I left the office, my steps quickening as I neared the elevator. I had to escape the suffocating air and focus on my work before guilt overwhelmed me. If I could concentrate everything on learning how to help others and perform in the manner expected, I would prove that leaving my family and friends was acceptable. Then, no one could blame me for my choices.

A hand darted between the slight opening of the elevator doors just as they were about to close with me inside. My eyes closed, and I blew out my breath. I had wanted to be alone, not bombarded with questions or concern or companionship of any kind.

Heavy footsteps forced my eyes open, and I scoffed at the sight of Mr. Smith entering the cab with me. He glanced at the unlit floor numbers, then back at me. "I thought you were going to the library."

"I... I am," I said, jabbing my index finger into the fourth-floor button. The doors slid shut, encasing me in the tomb with him. "You aren't watching the rest of the press conference?"

"Sandra and Jiong will keep me posted if anything relevant comes up."

"Great." Though his gaze burned through me, I kept mine solidly on the floor, my mind ticking off the ding of each floor.

The elevator shuddered to a stop, and I stepped forward when the doors parted.

"You can't push down your grief," Mr. Smith said from behind me.

I turned around and eyed him. He needed to follow that advice and quit taking the loss of his brother out on me.

"I know I'm not a good example," he said, "but you... I need your head here, with us."

Could he be any more of a jerk?

"I'm not trying to be a jerk," he said.

Clearly, he could read minds, too. I imagined myself flipping him off, but he didn't react. Maybe he couldn't hear my thoughts after all.

He reached in front of me, holding me back from exiting. His hand brushed against my abdomen, and I sucked in my breath with a sharp gasp, pulling my stomach back. Before I could say anything, he leaned over and opened a panel on the elevator wall, one I hadn't noticed. I prided myself on my perceptiveness, but this… I had missed it. Curiosity shut down my arguments against Mr. Smith keeping me hostage in the elevator, as I watched him depress an unlabeled button inside the panel.

"Just wait," he said, with an attempt at a smile, another peculiar sight.

The doors closed again, and weariness claimed my body. I leaned against the wall while I watched the numbers climb to five, six, and then they stopped flashing. I only knew of six floors, yet the elevator continued to climb.

After several seconds of no dinging to announce a new floor, I asked, "Are we going to bust through the ceiling?"

He laughed. "You'll see."

I didn't know what worried me more: the strange elevator not stopping, or Mr. Smith being in a decent mood. I shook my head, realizing I didn't even know what the outside of the building looked like… I had never bothered to ask what city, or even what state we were in. Did people walking past the complex see that there were no windows for floors between the sixth one and wherever we were going? Then again, I had yet to see any windows at all in the complex.

The thoughts disoriented my mind, and I leaned against the wall. I closed my brain for business; any other questions could potentially throw me into a drooling stupor.

The cab jerked slightly, then stopped. The doors parted, leading us to… darkness? Where the hell were we? I could make out the walls of the blackened hallway, but visibility was limited to that and Mr. Smith's outline.

He took my arm and placed my hand on his shoulder. "Stay with me."

I pinched his T-shirt so I wouldn't lose him, like a child

holding onto her parent in a crowd. From the moment he had guided me out of my hotel room, I had placed more trust in the man than I had in anyone else in my life. Even more than my family. More than Liz. And, I would continue to follow his lead, wherever it took me. If only he knew that he had become my lifeline in my crazy new reality.

"After you've been up here a few times," he said, "you'll get used to the dark."

"Maybe you should just call the electric company and pay the bill," I said.

A half-laugh, then, "There's a reason it's so dark."

We turned a corner to the left, and a sparkle of distant light caught my attention. A slight breeze down the hall brought with it the wondrous, fresh scent of the outdoors, something I hadn't experienced in a few days, something I had missed without knowing it. Excitement at going outside tickled my gut, and my steps picked up speed until I let go of Mr. Smith's shirt and moved in front of him. What would I see when we reached the end of the hall? Would I recognize the landscape? Or, would it be a strange new land?

The light brightened the closer we got to it, and I made out the outline of a balcony and railing. My brow pinched when I noticed the floor of the balcony was not made of wood, stone, brick, or tile, but of compacted dirt. The walls on either side of us transitioned to rock and dirt, pushing my curiosity to the brink. The city sounds I expected to hear did not rise above the silence coming from beyond the balcony. I turned to Mr. Smith to inquire further, but the smile playing on his lips told me to wait for the surprise.

Stepping onto the balcony, the sunset overcame me, stealing my breath and almost knocking me to the ground. It seeped through breaks in the mountain landscape, painting the brown land with deep oranges and yellows. Halfway to its nightly hideaway, the sun crested one of the high peaks, caressing it with warmth that seemed to disappear along the cool gusts of wind.

I crossed my arms to ward off any oncoming shivers and

moved to the edge of the railing. My head glided forward to see what laid below our feet. It only took a second to regret my curiosity. I grasped the iron in front of me and steadied my vertigo.

Mr. Smith's hand landed between my shoulder blades. "You okay?"

I pulled the night air into my lungs and looked up. "Shouldn't have done that," I said, a stifled laugh accompanying my words. "How far up are we?"

"About twelve thousand feet."

"Oh, just that high?" I glanced at him. "A little warning next time."

"Sorry, I forgot about your height thing." He removed his touch from my back and palmed the railing. "I thought the view would take your mind off everything else."

I lifted my head and realigned my thoughts. "It sure is gorgeous. But, where are we? I mean, where is the complex? Is it..." Realization dawned on me. "Is it built into a mountain?"

"Pretty ingenious if you ask me," he said, grinning. He pointed above our heads, and I noticed the top of the ledge curved down. "This is such a small opening that no one can see this shelf from the road, which is why there are no lights in the hall. We're completely hidden."

"Like a superhero cavern."

"It sure is." He leaned over, his forearms resting on the rail. "Brent used to call it our Batcave, even as an adult." His childlike excitement brought out another side of him, one that I liked much more than the gruff, always-tense man I'd come to know.

But, the mention of his brother reminded me of his – and my – loss, stirring me back to reality. I needed something more than a gorgeous view to remind me of my calling and reinforce staying.

"Tell me about someone you saved," I said.

He twisted his neck to look at me. "What do you mean?"

"I've read about people rescued from blood seekers back in, like, the fourteenth century. Tell me about someone you've saved since becoming a night stalker."

His eyes widened, and he shifted his gaze back to the landscape. "Oh, wow. There's been a lot. Not that I've personally saved, but that the team I've been on has saved." He squinted, and his mouth tweaked to the side as he thought. "I could tell you plenty of stories, but how about one of the more interesting missions I've been on?"

I smiled at the thought of a hopeful tale to comfort me. "That's perfect."

"There was this band back in the day. A garage band really, but they were pretty good. Probably had a great future ahead of them."

My expression dropped. "Don't tell me someone died."

He whipped his head toward me. "No, nothing like that. The lead singer of this band found out his cousin was in pretty deep with a sandman."

"A what? Sand… a sandman?"

"Nasty creature that feeds on the souls of children," he said. "Pray you never have to run up against one of those. I was around ten at the time, old enough to go on a hunt, and that sandman made me want to quit the life."

"Did your mark come in that early?"

"Nah, but I always knew I would be a night stalker. It's in my blood to do so. We traveled out to where these guys lived and got to know the band pretty well during our trip. Well, I did, that is. They played my kind of music."

"What kind of music is that?"

"Heavy metal. Betting you don't like that, huh?"

"Why? Because I'm write romance novels?" I laughed. "What, did you think I liked bubble gum pop or something?"

"I guess I didn't know what you would listen to."

"I just so happen like my music a bit on the heavy side."

"Oh, really? I have a pretty good collection of it, the older stuff, mostly. Anyway, this guy's cousin was near death when we got to him. My dad and the others were determined to save him, but more than that, we had to stop the sandman before he got to any other kids."

I turned to face him, completely engrossed in the tale. "Did you save him?"

"Of course, but that's not the real story. The lead singer of this band was there for everything – the entire mission. We had a talk with him, as usual. You know, don't tell anyone, keep it to yourself, etcetera. He didn't."

"What did he do?"

"He wrote a song about the experience."

My jaw dropped. "No, he didn't."

"It's so important that we keep these creatures under wraps. The world would go crazy if they even knew about blood seekers, let alone sandmen and the other monsters out there."

"What happened?"

"We had to shut the band down. Had the drummer's parents transferred with their job to another state, caused some chaos in the bassist's life, and some other things to ensure they would never start the band up again. We destroyed every copy of the song. It really sucked, but what were we supposed to do? Even though the lead singer promised he wouldn't release the song, it was only a matter of time. And, it was a great song. Would have been a hit for them."

"What was their name? Maybe I heard of them?"

"Doubt it. It was a bit before your time. Band's name was Metallica. Never forgot them. The song he wrote was called *Enter Sandman*. Pretty damn good."

"So, you heard the song? How did you manage that?"

He flashed a secretive grin. "My dad only *thought* we destroyed every copy. I managed to steal one before it went into the incinerator. I am now the proud owner of the only copy of *Enter Sandman* in the world, and no one outside the complex, including the high council, can find out."

The needle on my respect meter quivered up a few notches for the man. Maybe, he was a normal human being after all. "Do you know what happened to the band?"

"Yeah, I felt bad about breaking their band up, so I kept tabs on them over the years. The lead singer is an accountant in Oklahoma City. Wife, two kids, three dogs. Guitarist started a youth outreach program in Chicago. Changing lives through music, or something like that. Bassist plays in a Van Halen tribute band now out in Des Moines."

"No way," I said, laughing. "Poor guy."

"Hey, they aren't *bad*. Draws in some pretty good crowds. The drummer, though. I feel the worst about him."

"What happened to him?"

"He ended up going a little crazy. Broke into homes of famous drummers to steal their drum kits. Got caught within a year. Went to prison, got out, and started doing it again. He's in a mental institution now. Talking all kinds of nonsense about the monster that would have made him rich and famous."

"That's not good," I said. "So, even though the cousin didn't die, there was still some collateral damage?"

"You could say that, but we saved countless lives by disposing of that sandman."

"Have you had to do that with many people? Somehow stop someone from going public?"

"Too many," he said. "Have you ever heard of Bram Stoker?"

"Bram... uh, no."

"There's a reason you haven't. There's a book by him in the library you should read. It's a fictional account of a blood seeker. *Dracula*. Name of the book and the blood seeker."

"Dracula?" I choked on my laugh. "What an odd name."

"It does sound weird, doesn't it?" The corner of Mr. Smith's lips turned up. "Trust me, it was nothing like blood seekers really are, but we still had to stop it from circulation. Couldn't risk some strange fad about Draculas, or something where teenagers think it's cool to be a Dracula. Anything like that could eventually lead to the truth. It was a great book, though."

I smirked. "I didn't know you read books. You sure didn't seem to like them at all when we first met."

"Oh, I read. Just not trashy romance novels." He winked as a smile formed.

Shaking my head, I said, "I can't wait to read *Dracula*, but it does suck that a great book and a great song were never released to the masses. It's like we're robbing the world of things just so no one learns about monsters."

"I hate to say it, but the collateral damage of missed music careers and possibly groundbreaking novels is worth it in the end."

"You're right," I said, nodding. "It does sound awful."

"We've saved enough people to make it worth it."

I mulled it over for a few seconds before saying, "I don't know if I'm going to be able to contribute like I need to. I don't feel capable." An exasperated chuckle left my lips. "I can't even feel my legs right now, I'm so sore. There's no way I'm going to be in any condition to help. I would only slow you guys down."

"You're probably the best chronicler I've seen. Your connection with the chronicles is unbelievably strong, and you're growing at an abnormally fast pace. The other things will fall into place. When we do this mission, I'll be there, watching your every move, making sure you're safe." He moved closer and locked eyes with me. "I'm not going to let anyone hurt you. I swear that to you."

The connection between us solidified in that moment, one that had started when he confided to me about his brother, but seemed to disappear whenever we were at odds with each other. Or, maybe that was why I was always at irritated with him. To avoid anything other than an intense dislike of the man. Now, with the setting sun, the fresh air, and his honesty – and the close proximity of his body – I couldn't help but experience the true Mr. Smith. The one that awakened something inside of me, something long dead.

It both excited and frightened me.

His lips parted to say something else, but noise from the canyon below caught our attention. I looked over the edge. Distant headlights flooded a dirt road.

"Who's that?" I asked, my body tensing with fear.

"That, Madison, is the rest of our crew." He glanced back

at me and said, "The ones on the scouting mission."

"Oh, yeah," I said. "I suppose we should go find out what they learned."

He paused for a moment as he studied my face, then said, "I suppose we should." He turned to go back into the complex, leaving me confused about his personality – and our relationship – as I trailed after him.

Chapter Twenty

My head threatened to implode from the tension in the elevator ride down to the second floor. The awkwardness seemed to come only from me, as Mr. Smith appeared as collected as he normally did. At least his presence felt calm. I refused to look at his facial expression to confirm my theory.

Anger boiled inside me as I pushed aside thoughts of his little touches here and there, the intensity of his blue eyes, the way my heart had raced when he neared me. I had yet to think of him in terms outside of a grade-A, first-class, high-quality jerk. But, he broke through a part of me, and suddenly, I saw him as something different. As... *Spencer*. Whoever the hell that was.

My nails scratched furiously at an itch irritating my jawline. I squirmed a bit as imaginary hives broke out across my back. My right eye twitched to the same beat as my left thigh muscle, and my throat dried out, which made me cough. I must have been a sight: squirming and itching and twitching and coughing. But, my body wouldn't stop its allergic reaction to Mr. Smith.

The doors opened, and Mr. Smith told me to wait a moment while he grabbed Jia, Jiong, and Sandra. I pressed the "Open" button so hard that my knuckles ached after a few seconds of depressing it. The thought of abandoning him and going to the first floor by myself crossed my mind, but then I'd have to explain why I couldn't manage to keep the elevator doors opened for half a minute. At least when he returned, I wouldn't be stuck with him alone.

The four of them piled into the elevator, and I let go of the button. After pressing the button for the first floor, I shoved my body into the far, back corner, behind Sandra and beside Jiong, who separated me from Mr. Smith. To stem my mini freak-out, I told myself I was nervous because of the upcoming mission, the one that seemed even more real since the other night stalkers had returned. The intelligent part of my brain, the little dot of it that still existed, argued with me otherwise, but I ignored it.

When we landed on the first floor, I snuck out as fast as possible and moved as far away from Mr. Smith as I could get. My ears welcomed the sound of the voices in the lobby; I could keep avoiding Mr. Smith with that many distractions in one room.

Keira waited for us in the hall. She linked arms with me and pulled me close to her side. "How're you holding up?" she whispered.

Oh, that's right, I thought. *My parents found out I was dead today.* Somehow, I'd forgotten that, just as I kept forgetting about my life outside of the complex walls. What was wrong with me? To Keira, I said, "I'm fine, really."

"If you need to talk, you know where I am."

"Thanks, Keira."

"Did you like the view from the top?" she asked.

Did everyone know that Mr. Smith showed me the balcony? Embarrassment heated my cheeks, despite nothing having happened. Just the thought of being alone with him – and others knowing about it – was enough to throw me back into a tailspin.

"It's gorgeous," I said.

"I go up there whenever I've had a rough day," Keira said, oblivious to my desires to race back upstairs and jump off that cliff, all while enjoying the view. "You're welcome up there whenever you need to clear your head or whatever."

"I'll keep that in mind."

We reached the group in the lobby, and I glanced at the new faces. Each one appeared exhausted, some with bags under their eyes, some slouched over on a couch, but all five of the newcomers had grime, sweat, and even some blood on them. It told the story of a difficult scouting mission and hinted that the upcoming one to go after the blood seekers who killed Brent would be just as difficult, if not impossible.

Garrett sidled up to Keira, leaned around her, and waved at me. I smiled and lifted my hand, then turned my attention to Mr. Smith when he spoke.

"I know you're all tired, so we'll make this brief," Mr. Smith said, his voice hushing the quieter conversations.

"Before we start," Keira said, "this is our new chronicler, Mads."

I nodded as the others issued greetings. "Nice to meet you all."

"We'll get you introduced to everyone tomorrow when they've had a chance to rest up," Mr. Smith said. "Colin, why don't you give us the rundown."

A blond-haired man, lanky and lean, stood up from the armrest of the couch where he sat. "They're holed up about two hundred and fifty miles to the east. There's at least thirty of them, but two days ago, ten or so of them left and didn't return."

"We ran into a smaller group of them on the way back," another man said, his long, sandy-colored hair pulled into a ponytail at the base of his neck. He glanced at me before adding, "I'm Brady, by the way."

Without missing a beat, Mr. Smith asked, "What happened?"

"Rich, Brady, and I snuck up on them," Colin said, "while the others set up a blockade. Took out three, but the others got away. Went right past our blockade without us knowing it."

A woman in the back of the room raised her hand, as if in school.

"Morgan?" Mr. Smith pointed to her.

"Andre and I followed a few of them for an hour, but lost their trail."

A hulk of a man with shoulder-length dreadlocks in the middle of the group, who I assumed to be Andre, added, "There's something different about these ones, Spence. They're quicker, stronger, smarter."

"It's like a mutation," Colin said. "And, with that many blood seekers, it's going to be tough."

"Twenty left in the nest?" Mr. Smith asked.

"Give or take," Colin said. "But, we don't know when the others are returning."

"There could be more we didn't see," Morgan said. "We could be looking at thirty or possibly more."

"Spence," Keira said with a serious tone, "we've never gone up against that many before. We have to find a way to separate the nest."

No one spoke for several seconds while Mr. Smith appeared to contemplate the logistics of the job. When he did speak, it was with more authority than before. "Colin and Morgan, after you're cleaned up, let's meet to go over details. Jiong and Sandra, I want you to work with Rich and Andre on the coordinates and figure out the best plan of attack. Garrett, you and Jia can run communications with the other complexes. Find out if anyone can spare a few night stalkers. Let's also find out what others may know about a new breed of blood seekers."

Mr. Smith's eyes fell on me. "Madison, search the chronicles for any information about evolved blood seekers. If their abilities have changed and shifted in the past, maybe another chronicler notated that. Everyone else, please get some rest. We leave in five days to eradicate this nest."

The group broke up to head in their ordered directions without so much as a mutter about the short timeframe, especially given the new information from the scouting team. Was the man crazy? A nest of thirty or more blood seekers with only nine night stalkers and one amateur and out-of-shape chronicler? Maybe a few extra night stalkers if we were lucky? He should have indefinitely postponed the mission until we had better intel and more bodies for battle.

Still, I followed directions and headed straight to the library for my part of the research. It was going to be a long night.

Chapter Twenty-one

The odor of rotting flesh woke me from a deep sleep. I gagged on the smell and instinctively reached for my nose. My eyes flicked open to find Mr. Smith sitting across from me at a two-person table. The duct tape over his mouth didn't allow for any coherent words to emerge, and he struggled against the binds on his arms.

I jumped out of my seat and raced to his side. His head turned toward me, and I ripped the tape off his mouth. He exercised his jaw muscles while I worked on the ropes tying him to the chair. As I fumbled with the knots, my vision blurred, the stench in the room burning my eyes more than the sky snowing cotton in a field of blooms in springtime.

"We have to hurry," I said as I finished loosening the last knot. "I can smell them coming."

"It's too late," Mr. Smith said, his voice even and solid with conviction.

I moved back in front of him and crouched beside him, one knee on the ground. "No, it's not. They aren't here right now."

My gaze wandered around the room, as if I needed to prove to myself we were alone. No one – no blood seekers or any other creatures – invaded our space, but I recognized the room as the café where I met Mr. Smith for the fake interview. At least, all the furnishings remained the same. The dusty plastic vines, and even the white walls were off a few shades. Just enough to notice the dullness of it all.

"Doesn't matter," Mr. Smith said. "You need to leave without me."

I glanced him over, and no obvious wounds to rendered him unable to leave with me. "I'm not leaving you. Get up."

He didn't move a muscle.

"Get up!" I rose to my feet and tugged on his arm, trying to pull him to a standing position. His dead weight, however, made the attempts futile. "Why aren't you getting up? We have to go!"

"I'm not going anywhere," he said, his voice still at a normal level without a hint of anxiousness at the situation. "I need to stay here and distract them so you can get away."

"I can't do this without you, Spencer."

His eyes widened, and he finally rose from the seat, but not to leave. Taking my hands in his, he said, "You've never called me that before."

My lips parted with a sharp gasp, and I stepped away from him, but he held onto my hands. "We have to go now. They're going to be here any minute, and—"

"This is a dream, Madison. They don't have to come here if we don't want them to."

"A dream?" I shook my head. "But, everything is so real." Right down to the warmth of his hands surrounding mine, the eager flapping of butterfly wings in my stomach, and the irregular beating of my heart. I wriggled my hands free, uneasy at the emotions his touch stirred inside me.

"I promise you," he said, "only a dream."

Phantom hives broke out across my stomach, neck, and chest again, but I resisted the urge to rake my fingernails over them. Dream or not, I didn't want to perform the crazy lady scratch dance for him, one where I'd writhe in an effort to relieve the itching while my face contorted like I'd sucked on a thousand lemons.

Instead, I pleaded with him once more to leave. "I can't stop them from coming. Just go with me. Please. There's no reason why you can't."

"One day, you'll understand that sacrifices need to be made. I'm not going to let what happened to Brent happen to you."

I shook my head and plopped down in my seat. "Then, I'm not leaving, either. I can't let you stay here, knowing that you'll be killed."

He huffed and stared at me for a moment. On the other side of the table, he grabbed the top of the chair and carried it over to me, setting it down so it faced my seat. He sat down and leaned over, his elbows on his knees, uncomfortably close to me once more. "You will leave," he said. "But, we have some time before they come."

My frustration with him boiled over. "What do you want with me?"

He responded without blinking. "The same thing you want with me."

My throat dried out, but I managed to say, "I don't want anything with you – from you."

"I think we both know that's not true."

"No, I know *it's* true. From the minute we met, you made it clear that you have a strong dislike for me. Even when you're attempting to play nice, you're not. We can barely say two words to each other without—"

His hands found mine again and encased them. "I shouldn't do that to you," *he said.* "I should have welcomed you into this life, but I didn't know how. I had just lost Brent, and I wasn't ready for a new chronicler to come in and take his spot. Pushing you away is so much easier, especially considering—"

"Considering what? That we'd likely kill each other if left unattended?"

He smirked, but his face instantly sobered. "Considering that from the moment I saw you, I..." *He averted his gaze to our hands and lowered his voice.* "I haven't stopped thinking about you."

My racing heartbeat – maybe in conjunction with his? – pounded against the veins in my hands, coursing through my wrists and up my arms. The air thickened in my lungs, constricting my airways. "I can't... I mean, I don't..." *The words wouldn't come, wouldn't even form in my mind so they could find a way to my mouth.*

"You push me away, too."

I closed my eyes and ran my tongue over my dry lips. I did push him away. Every chance I got. Distance made tolerating him so much easier. At least that was what I had told myself. Maybe there were other reasons, ones I didn't want to admit to anyone.

"It's time we're honest with each other," *he said.*

Honesty didn't work for me in this situation, and probably never would. "Why do we have to go to that extreme?"

"You know why."

What is my subconscious trying to tell me in this dream? I wondered, but I didn't voice my thoughts. "What's the point? You said it yourself. This is only a dream. It does neither of us any good to talk about this here and now. And, talking about it out there in the real world wouldn't work, either. I don't want to know how you feel about me, and

I sure as hell don't want to know how I feel about you. Things need to stay the way they are between us, and if we eventually kill each other, so be it."

"Maybe, I need *to talk about it," he said. "Maybe, I've been trying to deny that I feel anything for you, and that's not working for me anymore. If I tell you this in my dream, then I can keep suffocating it when you're really in front of me."*

I opened my mouth to respond, but stopped. His *dream?* Why did he think—

The floor shifted beneath my feet, followed by the walls quivering in fear of nature's wrath. I'd experienced several minor earthquakes since moving to California, enough to lessen my initial anxieties over them, but this one managed to rattle my soul.

Mr. Smith ripped his hands from mine as he jumped up, pushing his chair back. It screeched across the floor, then wobbled until it crashed to the ground.

I also shot out of my seat and grabbed the table for support. The tremor ceased, but a stench floated through the room, accosting my senses. I had known the moment was coming, that time when we'd no longer be safe in the café, but Mr. Smith's inability to understand "timing" with his uninvited talk of emotions and the fluffy stuff of life had distracted me from impending danger. I'd all but forgotten the duct tape over his mouth and rope binding him to the chair when I first awoke in the room – or drifted off to sleep, if this were truly a dream, something of which I was still unsure.

My neck whipped from left to right as far as it could, searching for the source of the foul odor, but the café remained empty, save for the two of us. I looked to Mr. Smith for guidance, but found him partway across the room, near a freestanding white column wrapped in plastic grapevine, searching for his own answers.

Something in the air swelled between us, a curious motion as if an invisible object halfway between the floor and ceiling pushed outward, trying to escape a prison. The movement stopped, and I walked toward it with deliberate steps and narrowed eyes. Unsure of what exactly I had seen, I followed my instincts and lifted my trembling hand as I neared the spot. I reached out to touch the air, but my fingers grazed an unseen wall made of a squishy, gelatin-like substance. I pulled back my hand and jumped as ripples branched out in the air, the same as it would if I had disturbed the calm surface of water.

Mr. Smith turned to see the barrier. He raced to it, but resistance met him when he reached the wall. His fists pounded against it to no avail. Whatever separated us was much too strong.

Fear crushed my throat as a familiar pull reached into my soul, and I bowed my head in defeat. I didn't have to turn around to know Dark Man, Mullet Man, and possibly others stood behind me. Mr. Smith called out to me, tried to warn me, but there was no escape.

I rotated and faced my fate. Five blood seekers, including Dark Man and Mullet Man, waited for me across the café, in front of the emergency exit door.

"I knew you'd find me again, my pet," Dark Man said, the words rolling through the air like a hypnotic breeze.

"It's a dream," I said.

"That might be so," he said, "but you still found me here. Come to me. It's time for me to taste you again."

Mr. Smith's muted calls to me did nothing to halt my puppeteered walk toward Dark Man. Beyond my control, my limbs moved purposefully, slowly, as if I were a reluctant bride strolling down the aisle to meet my groom in a forced wedding. The tears dampening my cheeks reflected the fading part of my mind that, unsuccessfully, ordered my body to stop.

When I reached him, I lifted my head and gazed into his eyes with love and longing, as if we'd made it to our wedding night. The backs of his fingers stroked my cheek, and I nuzzled into his touch as a faint smile crossed my lips.

His other hand climbed up my bare arm, and he fingered the strap of my tank top, the one I had fallen asleep in. He pulled it off my shoulder and aroused the nerve endings in my skin, filling me with desire. All other sounds in the room ceased as his fingertips teased me from my shoulder up my neck and to my jaw.

Mullet Man stepped up and offered Dark Man an unremarkable dagger. I tilted my head to the side, and Dark Man pressed the blade to the meat between my shoulder and neck. The pain enthralled me, as I knew what would follow. He lowered his head, and his tongue snaked out over my skin, licking the blood dripping down my upper arm.

He stopped long enough to look at me. My blood on his lips stirred my need for him, and my lips parted as my eyes closed.

"You are the most delectable creature I've ever tasted, my pet," he said.

His mouth fell to my wound, and he sucked hard enough to lift the skin around the cut. A sharp pinch of his teeth into my flesh made me grimace, but only for a second as I fell deeper under his spell. I slipped into a waking coma of sorts, and my legs seemed to disappear from beneath me. Someone caught me from behind so I wouldn't fall, and Dark Man continued his sensual feast.

I never wanted it to end.

When it did, I begged for him to continue, but he shushed me. "I don't want to drain you," *he said.* "You need to get your strength back."

Whoever stood behind me and Dark Man helped to turn me around. Crouched to the floor behind the invisible wall, Mr. Smith's turmoil shone through in his creased brow, pinched face, and glassy eyes.

"It's your turn," Dark Man whispered in my ear. *"Blood from a night stalker is quite a treat."*

Remembering the sinful deliciousness of Liz's blood in my last dream, I smiled. Mr. Smith would taste a thousand times better.

"Once the virus is in you, we can bring him with us so you can feed from him whenever you want."

My tongue snaked across my lips in anticipation, but the word "virus" struck a part of me that remained human. I didn't want to be infected. I didn't want my insides to decay, and I didn't want to feed from anyone for survival, let alone Mr. Smith.

Mr. Smith... I looked across the barrier at him, his pleading eyes, concerned lines around his mouth. His words reverberated in my mind. "I haven't stopped thinking about you." *I hadn't stopped thinking about him, either. I wanted to hate the man, wanted to push him away with everything I had, but another part of me knew, eventually, I'd have to face that I felt something for him. No matter how that "something" was defined.*

I took a step away from Dark Man, toward Mr. Smith. One foot, then the other, I made my way across the room. Dark Man protested from behind me, but I blocked out the sound. I couldn't risk him controlling me again.

The gelatinous, clear wall separating me from Mr. Smith disappeared as I passed through it. Maybe, there had never been a barrier; it was imagined, possibly inserted in our minds by Dark Man.

"Madison!"

I turned at Dark Man's voice. One last glimpse at the monster I had almost become in my dream.

"You will be with me soon. There's no escaping our bond, my pet."

I wanted to respond, but determined that engaging him further would only end badly. Instead, I faced Mr. Smith and accepted his outstretched hand. A flash of light blinded me, then darkness.

Chapter Twenty-two

I don't know how long I remained curled up in bed, wide-eyed and numb from my nightmare. My body paralyzed, the thought of leaving the comfort of my covers terrified me. Even if fear didn't have me stuck in one position, my sore muscles from the torturous workout the day before had no intentions of moving an inch. I had no choice but to lay still and analyze my dreams.

Something about them… they didn't feel like normal dreams, no matter how many of the others in the complex told me they also suffered from nightmares. These were as if reality had seeped into my sleep, as if everything had truly happened. As if Mr. Smith had been with me, as if he had said…

I shook my head and snapped back to the present. The blood seekers were bad enough without Mr. Smith rambling on about emotions and feelings and all those wretched things. Outside of contempt for taking his brother's place as the new chronicler, some tolerance toward me had shone through the cracks of his hard exterior. I figured that was as good as it could get with us. Tolerate each other long enough to get the job done and nothing more. Never anything more.

Then again, for a romance writer, I never really dated. I wasn't gushy in real life, didn't care for romantic gestures. No one would ever hold a boombox outside of my bedroom window. I would be way too cranky about the noise. Flowers just died, which was what all of my six short-lived relationships since high school had done. And, who needed diamonds? Much too flashy for my taste. No, if I ever married, it would be to someone low-key, someone who understood that while I could write the heck out of love scenes, I had no use for them in real life. But, finding someone to tolerate me long enough to love me was a foreign concept.

There was that word again. "Tolerate." Mr. Smith tolerated me. He could snap back, too. Match my sarcasm with something wry. Or, just ignore me altogether. Abilities I knew I would have to find in any man that stood a chance in my life.

Nope. There were no feelings there. Either way. Not from me, not from him. In fact, placed together in a room, love and even "like" couldn't breathe. Our mutual frustration and anger with each other blew way too much carbon dioxide on any positive emotions outside of "tolerance." Love couldn't survive around us. Definitely not *with* us.

Satisfied I had straightened out my confusion about Mr. Smith, I turned my thoughts to the blood seekers. In particular, Dark Man. In my nightmares, he had a way of controlling me. Forcing me to gravitate toward him, and in a most disturbing way. My complacency with him, my *compliance*... while it scared me, it also saddened me. Was I such a weak soul that something evil could turn me so easily?

I would be face-to-face with a blood seeker soon enough. Mr. Smith's mission to avenge his brother guaranteed it. Surely, when I saw one, when I was close enough that the odor of decay overwhelmed me, I would resist anything that came my way. They couldn't control my mind, and they wouldn't turn me into one of them.

A knock on my door startled me into a sitting position. The door opened, and Keira came through, bubbly and dressed in spandex shorts and a tight workout tank. I groaned and flopped back down on my pillow.

"Come on," she said, drawing out the last word. "You know you want to hit the gym hard today."

"No, I really don't," I said. "I honestly don't know if my

muscles even work still. I think they're all broken. No, more like shattered."

She bounced down on the side of my bed and sighed. "It gets easier, I promise. After a week, you'll crave working out."

"Easy for you to say. I mean, look at you."

She broke into laughter. "You think I always had muscle? Oh, when I first came here, I was in worse shape than you. I was pudgy in all the right places."

"The milkshakes, huh?" I asked, sitting up.

"Damn milkshakes plus greasy diner food all the time."

Her smile brought my mood back around to a good place. I had only known her for a few days, but it seemed like much longer. She could already read me, already knew how to handle me, and her presence warmed my soul.

"Let's get the gym out of the way now," she continued, "then you can head off to the library for the day."

"He's really pushing this mission through fast."

"Do you blame him?"

I paused before answering. "No, but I'm worried. Probably just anxiety over it being my first mission. Four days from now… doesn't seem like enough prep time, even for an experienced team."

"It is aggressive," Keira said.

"Do you ever get scared?"

Lips pursed, she looked down. "Not for myself. I know this life is dangerous, and if it's my time, that's the way it is. I just can't lose Garrett. That would kill me faster than any blood seeker."

I reached for her hand and squeezed it. "I couldn't imagine that kind of fear."

"Losing Brent was hard enough. Losing anyone here… They're my family." She raised her head and smiled. "They're your family now, too."

Her words rang through my mind, and I knew she spoke the truth. Keira was more than a friend; she was the sister I never had. Our marks united us, just as it bonded me to everyone in the complex, and even those in other complexes.

Despite being an author and being part of that community, I never experienced true belonging. Like if I disappeared one day, I wouldn't be missed by anyone other than my family and friends. But this... this was different in so many ways. I was *born* into this life, even if I hadn't been called to it until now. I had finally discovered my reason for being.

Not wanting to dwell on the topic, I asked, "Do I have time to take a shower before the gym?"

"Not today," she said, getting off the bed. "You can after, but I want to get you in there now so you have more time in the library for all your research."

I groaned again, louder than when she first came into my room. "I'll throw on some clothes." I climbed out of bed. "Can I at least brush my teeth?"

She wrinkled her nose. "Yes. *Please*, please do."

Laughing, I headed to the restroom to get minty fresh.

Chapter Twenty-three

"So, Spence took you up to The Ridge last night." Playful accusation and insinuation underscored Keira's tone.

I ignored it and kept jogging beside her. "Is that what it's called? The Ridge?"

"Yeah. It's beautiful up there." We ran in silence for a moment before she added, "You know, that's where Garrett proposed to me."

My lips tightened. I was still recovering from too weird of a dream for all this romance talk. "It was nice to get my mind off everything with my family and friends."

"I remember when the police found my 'body.' One of my cousins ended up cremating me. None of my immediate family showed up to my wake. A few people from the diner where I worked decided to make an appearance."

I faltered in my running and came to a stop.

Keira skidded in front of me and turned around. "What is it?" she asked.

"I'm just sorry, that's all. I've been doing nothing but blabbering on about my family, and yet I wish you'd had as good of a family as I did."

She smiled and shook her head. "Nothing to be sorry about. I am right where I'm supposed to be, and I couldn't be happier. Maybe if I'd had a great family, I wouldn't have been called to be a night stalker."

Her outlook on her life gave me hope that I could find the same positivity in my situation. "How long did it take you to get used to all this?" I asked.

"Several months and a few missions. You're doing much better accepting everything than I did."

"I don't feel like it," I said. "Every time something happens – a press conference or finding my 'body,' I think I'm going to crack. I think that's why Mr. Smith took me to The Ridge last night. Get my mind off everything."

"Sure," she said with a smirk. "I just want to know what's going to happen when you stop calling him 'Mr. Smith.' That'll be interesting."

"What are you—"

"You weren't dating anyone when you came here, were you?"

"I... I don't..." I shook my head and realigned my thoughts. "I don't really date."

"What? Of course you date. You're a romance author."

"I know, and Liz would kill me if I admitted the truth to anyone. I'm supposed to give off an appearance of having all these romantic relationships and the occasional clandestine rendezvous. But, dating doesn't appeal to me much. I've maybe had six boyfriends since high school. All short-term."

"Don't ever tell Garrett that," she said. "He apparently sees the image of you that your publicist painted."

I laughed. "I don't know why it's such a big deal. It's not like a thriller or mystery writer kills people before they write about it. No one cares if they lead non-murderous lives."

"I'm with you," she said, "but Garrett is a super-fan of yours. In case you didn't pick that up earlier."

"I love Garrett," I said. "He's the perfect fan, but so down-to-earth. He doesn't blow my author status out of proportion."

"Not to you, he doesn't. After you guys chatted the other night, he was fangirling all over the place. Wouldn't let me sleep."

My stomach rocked with a hard laugh, and I doubled over.

Keira joined in, just as tickled at her effeminate husband. "You're definitely the man in that relationship, huh?" I asked.

"You have *no* idea. I drink whiskey, he prefers red wine. He yells for me when a remote doesn't work or even when a light bulb needs changing. I'm addicted to those true crime shows and football, and – well, you know, he watches every desperate housewife and love-seeking reality show ever created." She rolled her eyes and leaned in to me. "Between us, I think he's ecstatic you're here so he can finally have someone to watch television with."

"Don't worry," I said. "I have no problems indulging him in all those shows. I'm just glad I don't have to give them up."

"Thank you," she said in a loud whisper. "Thank you, thank you, *thank* you."

I laughed again. "I guess we have to get back to our workout. I really want to get to the library soon, you know, before my legs fall off."

Chuckling, she said, "I don't think that's ever happened here, but I know how you feel. By my day two here, I wanted my legs to fall off just so I wouldn't have to work out ever again."

"I don't suppose the doctor here would perform unnecessary amputations?"

"Not today," she said and took off running.

I rushed to catch up to her, my muscles screaming with every movement. I couldn't envision a time when my body wouldn't ache, but Keira had promised I would soon crave the exercise. The only thing I craved in that moment was a shot of tequila with a candy bar chaser.

The half-mile track was built around the gym, most of it behind walls with only a large opening to exit the track. The corridors forced the runner to follow through with the distance. Markers on the wall relayed our progress with the run, and I was pleased to see the final marker before the exit.

"Can we stop here?" I asked, already knowing the answer. Like a loquacious, annoying child on a road trip, I'd voiced the question at least four other times during our run.

"We've only done two miles," Keira said, laughing at me. "We've got three more to go, but I'll make it four if you don't quit asking."

I groaned, but kept my speed up to match hers. As if I had something to prove – more to myself than anyone else – I would keep going until we either finished the full five miles or I passed out. That would be the only way I'd quit. With my first mission merely days away, I had no choice but to get in shape fast if I wanted to stay alive. No more brownie thighs and cotton candy midriff for this sweets junkie.

We rounded the corner, and I peeked out at the gym to see two men sparring without protective gear. Keira stopped running, and I did as well. I swallowed hard as I recognized the men as Mr. Smith and Garrett – both shirtless. I averted my gaze and prayed Keira would immediately start running again. Instead, she wandered into the gym, toward a bench near the men.

"Can't we finish our run?" I asked. "I really want to get to the library."

"I love it when they spar," she said. "I hope you don't mind." She glanced at my face and said, "Heating up from the run?"

The crimson coating my skin seemed to boil, even more so when she pointed it out. I didn't want to see Mr. Smith without a shirt. It was *Mr. Smith*. Just this… *thing* I had to deal with occasionally. Nothing more to see there.

"Uh, yeah," I said. I motioned to the track. "Come on. Let's finish this thing."

"I think it's more beneficial for you to watch this sparring. Then, we can get back to running. Nothing wrong with taking a break, and you might learn something." She winked at me.

I hated her in that moment, as friends often do. But, despite knowing her motives weren't only for me to learn by watching, I followed her to the bench. Once settled on the hard wood, which dug into my tailbone in a most uncomfortable manner, I leaned over with my elbows on my knees. Lowering my head, I watched sweat drip from my forehead onto the floor. Anything to avoid looking at Mr. Smith.

"You won't learn anything if you don't watch," she said.

Frustrated, I looked up to get her to stop talking. Keira was much more intuitive than I wanted to give her credit for, and I didn't want her to say anything more about me and Mr. Smith. I didn't even want to hear our names in the same conversation.

As the men traded punches, I glanced down Mr. Smith's body, purely unintentionally, and caught sight of the tattoo. Black ink sprawled across his side and ribs. I couldn't make out the image, but it seemed to be a symbol of sorts.

"What's the tattoo?" I asked Keira.

"Ah," she said. "The tattoo of shame."

I perked up with curiosity. "Sounds like a good story."

"Garrett has the same one, but it's on his right side, which is why you can't see it too well. When their marks came in, Garrett and Spence were called to be night stalkers, they decided to get a couple fake IDs and get tattoos to commemorate it. Can you translate the tattoo?"

I squinted and stared at Mr. Smith's side, his muscles contracting under the ink. He moved a bit, giving me a glimpse of the rest of the tattoo. "It's a night stalker symbol."

Keira smiled. "You *are* good. It's the official symbol of The Order of the Night Stalker."

"That's not something I'd think they'd be allowed to get tattooed."

"You're right. When their parents discovered it, the high council had a nightmare on their hands. They were called to headquarters to answer to the council."

"They must have been horrified."

"Some council members wanted them completely removed from the ranks and kicked out of the complex, but because Spence and Garrett were still minors, there weren't many people that could stand the thought of them being homeless. They had no family outside the complex. Plus, their family has a long history in this life. They're kinda royalty around here. So, instead of banishment, they were sanctioned with heavy workloads for the next year."

"Why didn't the council demand the tattoos be removed?"

"They debated that, too, but that would have involved another person to remove them, and there were too many loose ends to clean up already."

"That's insane," I said. "I don't really see Mr. Smith as a rulebreaker."

"Those two boys are a disaster together, even as adults, but they're the best of friends."

Remembering the story Mr. Smith had told me about the band with the song about the sandman, I asked, "What happened to the tattoo artist?"

"The council arranged it so he closed his business. He'd had an uncle die a few months earlier, one who had no wife or kids. They created a fake insurance policy from a fake company leaving half a million dollars to the tattoo artist. Then, they opened an opportunity for him to get a shop down in Australia."

"What about his portfolio? Don't tattoo artists take pictures of great tattoos?"

"Yes, and he did. That's why just before he started packing to go to Australia, his shop had an unfortunate fire. He lost everything, including his portfolio."

"Good thing he had that half million dollars then," I said.

"And, a much better fire insurance policy than he realized. He was set up real nice."

"I can't believe how much work goes into keeping monsters and The Order a secret."

"It's a constant battle," Keira said, sighing. "Headquarters has a whole department dedicated to just that. Monitoring people who have been saved from a creature, watching news reports, reading blogs, social media. If they find something, they have to devise a way to make the problem go away without being suspicious."

A disturbing thought lanced my mind. "They've never killed anyone who came out about creatures, have they?"

"No, they would never do that. But, some people need a

bit more convincing to keep their mouths shut." She nudged me with her elbow, then pointed to the guys. "Watch and learn."

I looked up right as Mr. Smith turned his head and noticed me. I squirmed on the bench, those damned imaginary hives returning. As much as I'd tried to forget it, my ridiculous dream from the night before replayed in my mind.

"Maybe I've been trying to deny that I feel anything for you, and that's not working for me anymore."

I scratched at my neckline as I recalled his words. In waking hours, they seemed to be more of a nightmare than Dark Man.

"If I tell you in my dream, then I can keep suffocating it when you're really in front of me."

"Shut up," I mumbled. Grimacing, I noticed Keira looking at me from the corner of my eye. I had meant to only think it. I gave her a fake smile and said, "Just ignore me. Having one of those days, I guess."

"Well, okay then," she said, and focused back on the men sparring.

"Why don't they use padding?" I asked.

"They've always been like this. Brent, too. They claim it makes the practice more real for them."

"I bet there's lots of bruising later."

"They try not to hit each other too hard, but yeah. Some days, they come out of here looking like they were jumped in a back alley."

"I get the concept, but still can't believe they go to those lengths."

"Yeah, Garrett said that Spence came out of these things with more than one broken nose as a teenager."

Immediately, I had to search Mr. Smith's face to see for myself. Sure enough, a small, irregular bump at the bridge of his nose revealed the trauma of at least one break.

Mr. Smith's fist lashed out toward Garrett, striking him in the jaw with a loud *thud*.

"Hey, hey, boys," Keira called out. "Take it down a few

notches. Don't need you guys in medical before this mission."

"How about you two join us?" Garrett asked. "You're getting a bit rusty as it is, babe."

Keira jumped to her feet and rushed to the men. "You wanna see rusty?" She stepped in front of Mr. Smith on the mat, who backed away.

As she jabbed at Garrett with her fists, Mr. Smith walked toward me. I wanted to sink into the bench or find a hidden exit beneath it. If I were quick, maybe my sore body could get to the track before he reached me, and I could disappear in the corridors for at least a half mile.

No such luck.

"Why don't we have a go?" he asked, standing above me.

"A... what? You mean... oh. Um, well—"

"And, here I thought writers were chock-full of words."

The most irritating man ever. Human, even. In fact, in that moment, I was willing to bet that no person in future generations could possibly outdo him in the category of annoying.

"Well," I said, "I wasn't sure if you were asking me or ordering."

"Not really much of a difference between the two."

I reluctantly rose from the bench, though I remained slumped over. Crossing my arms, I said, "That's what I was afraid of."

"Let's go over here," he said, gesturing to the mat behind him.

Arms still folded over my chest, I stood in front of him on the mat. "You do realize I'm barely able to move right now."

"Just like most people who first get here," he said. "When you grow up in this life, you're working out as early as three years old. But, I know that those who are called here aren't always health nuts."

"There's no way I'll be in shape in time for this mission."

"No one expects you to be. I just need you as prepared as possible so I can do my job of protecting you. If something happens and I'm detained by a blood seeker, you might be on your own for a few minutes."

My anxiety level shot up so high so fast that it probably orbited the Earth. "I... I'm not ready to be on my own in any capacity."

He stepped forward, his gaze never wavering from mine. "I am going to keep you safe. I promise you. But, I still have to try to get you ready."

I nodded and looked away. My mind hadn't truly accepted that I would soon face down blood seekers. I silently vowed to do my best to follow every direction he gave and to put my all into these workouts. My survival instinct demanded it.

"What do we do first?"

"You're always going to try to be on the offensive," he said, "but that doesn't mean you falter in defense. Put your arms up and try to spread your legs just enough so you can center your core."

I lifted my fists, but shifted my unnatural stance several times, trying to find a comfortable position.

Mr. Smith walked behind me and wrapped his arms around me, his hands underneath mine. He arranged my fists. Stepping back, his fingers grazed my outer thighs as he directed me on where to move my legs. He placed his hands on my waist. "Stay tight in your core. This is your center and will keep you in balance. Lower your body just a bit so your legs are bearing more weight."

"It's time we're honest with each other."

I cringed away from him as bits of my dream assaulted me again, but his body was still much too close to mine. I knew my trembling body shook through his hands to *his* core. Was it normal to touch someone like this when training them? Outside of Physical Education in high school, which I proudly passed with a C-minus grade, I hadn't done much in the way of activity. Unless I counted the hours of exercising my carpal tunnel syndrome while pounding away on a keyboard or accelerating the symptoms of arthritis in my right hand while signing books for hours on end.

Of course, before my journey down this rabbit hole, I

probably wouldn't have minded an attractive man showing me how to stand. It would have been the highlight of my year. After my dream last night, however, I didn't want anyone touching me in any way for any reason – especially not *him*.

Mr. Smith stood in front of me again and studied me. "Move your right leg an inch to the left." After I complied, he said, "How does that feel?"

Grateful his hands were no longer on me, I said, "Fine, I guess."

"You're cowering."

I stared at him as if he spoke a foreign language.

"You're scared," he said, clarifying for me. "I can sense it, and blood seekers will, too. They'll take advantage of your fear."

"I'm not…" I started, then stopped. "Okay, yeah. Last time we did this, you hit me. I don't think I'm going to be where I need to be by this mission, and I'm a little freaked out about these blood seekers."

"That's okay. A bit of fear is healthy and needed, but we have to get you to the point where your fear is minimal. Seeing them in real life for the first time can be terrifying. It's the smell, more than anything. The death and decay coming from them… it's hard to explain."

"I smelled them at the hotel." I lowered my hands, but kept my legs in the ready position.

"That was nothing," Mr. Smith said. "When they nest, when there's more than two of them, it can be overwhelming."

"How do they manage to get around if they smell so awful?"

"They go out during the night mostly. Daytime is too risky."

"So, do we hit them when they're asleep during the day?"

"They don't sleep. They're dead inside, so all those humanly functions don't pertain to them."

My mind reverted back to my strange dream and the way Dark Man spoke to me. "What about emotion? If they're dead, do they still have feelings and things like that?"

"If they did, they probably wouldn't be able to kill like they do, but there's some sort of loyalty to their nest. That would require some emotion."

"Okay, you're freaking me out just a bit more now, so let's get on to you hitting me or whatever it is we're doing here. Keira's gonna make me run three more miles, and I still have a full day ahead of me in the library. And, then Garrett and I have a date with some sports wives later tonight and—"

"What? Sports wives?"

"It's a television show we both watch."

"Should've guessed. I swear, if he wasn't married already... Nah, scratch that. You two get along too well to be together. You're more like his idol than anything."

"I shouldn't be *anyone's* idol." I raised my fists again. "Let's get this over with."

"Okay," he said, taking his own stance. "When I punch out..." He demonstrated with a slow movement toward my face.

I jumped back.

"I'm not going to hit you," he said and gestured for me to move forward. "I'll feign a punch, and you defend it."

"How do I do that?"

"Just knock it away." At my confused look, he said, "No one is going to expect you to be battle-ready for the mission. Eventually, we'll get you trained up right. For now, you need to do what you can to be effective during a confrontation."

He pushed his fist toward me again, and I used the outside of my wrist to deflect it away from my face.

"Good," he said. "How did it feel?"

"I hit my bone a bit, but it's okay."

"Then, let's stick with that, but avoid hitting your wrist bone. Again."

We practiced the same defense over and over, then switched hands. After a few minutes of that, he randomly used each fist, coming at me faster with each hit.

"It's really not that bad," I said when we stopped.

"You have good reflexes, which will come in handy."

I glanced over at Keira and Garrett, who were in full-battle mode. My eyes widened. "I don't think I'll *ever* get that good."

"You will," Mr. Smith said. "You have to. When you're in a fight for your life, you won't be able to ask them to slow down, and there are no do-overs."

"You know, in gym class, when we had to pick teams, they wouldn't even *say* my name, even though I was the last kid standing," I said, chuckling. "Are you sure you want me on your team?"

He sharpened his stare, and his expression sobered. "There's no one better for this job than you, Madison." The Mr. Smith from my dream suddenly stood in front of me, the ooey-gooey one with all his sentiments and honesty.

I much preferred the jerk.

Swallowing hard, I asked, "Okay, what's next?"

He cleared his throat, quite possibly aware of his change in tone and mood. "Let's do a few more combinations like that, then move on to kicks."

I followed his lead through another hour of training, surprised at how quickly I picked up everything he taught me. Could it be part of my new superpowers? Or, maybe I'd had these abilities all along. It just took the fear of succumbing to blood seekers to bring it out in me.

Mr. Smith spun in front of me with a rapid kick to my midsection. I successfully blocked it, then panicked at what to do next. My foot flailed up, right to his crotch. He grunted, but I didn't have a chance to apologize. Within seconds, I lay flat on my back, Mr. Smith straddling me with my arms pinned above my head.

I struggled against his hold, but relinquished my fight. His strong face said I'd never escape. The occasional drop of sweat dripped from his forehead and hit my face, and I was all-too aware of his body against mine.

Quashing my romance-writer brain, I searched for a way out from under him. "I give up," I said, hoping he'd move aside. "You win."

"Never go for that area unless you're sure you're gonna hit

your target," he said from above me.

My skin burned with another deep flush. "I didn't mean to... I panicked and didn't know what to do, and my foot just flew—"

"Don't panic next time," he said. "As soon as you lose track of what you're doing, you die." He climbed off me and stood up, reaching his hand down to help me.

I ignored his gesture of goodwill and got to my feet. Brushing off my yoga pants, I said, "I think it's time for me to hit the library." I looked to my right and saw Keira and Garrett still engulfed in sparring. There was no way I was going to stop her and risk her forcing me to run three more miles. "Tell Keira for me, will you?"

"I'll come get you for lunch," he said.

"Not eating lunch today. Too much research to do." Before he could protest, I added, "I had a large breakfast, and I'll eat good at dinner. I swear."

He nodded, apparently not wanting to launch into an argument over me getting too lost in the chronicles to eat. "I'll come get you for dinner, then."

I lifted my hand in a quick wave and stumbled out of the gym. In the elevator, I depressed the button to go down to my room for a shower. I clasped my hands together to try and cease my sudden trembling, and a rush of cold sweat coated the back of my neck. Aftereffects of adrenaline, I told myself, but it was more than that.

So much more.

Chapter Twenty-four

"Argh!"

My vocalized frustration summed up my day in the library. I had gone back and forth, finding book after book, but none gave me any clues as to the possible evolution of blood seekers.

I thrust my elbows onto the desk, and my head plopped onto my open palms. Meant to be deep, calming breaths, several loud sighs escaped my lungs. My jaw tightened, and my bottom teeth clamped down on my upper lip.

The most important job I had – providing crucial information to night stalkers for upcoming missions – and I was failing on my first assignment. I internally pummeled myself at my incompetence. Though part of me said there may be nothing in the chronicles and that was why I couldn't find it, something else told me that I had to keep searching. That the information was there, *somewhere*, in the library.

Lifting my head, my arms thudded against the desk. I looked at my mini-collection of fourteen books piled up and shook my head.

"Your problem is you're trying too hard."

I hated having Mr. Smith in my head, both in waking and dreaming hours, and it irritated me more that he was right about so many things. However, in that moment, I needed his candor more than I realized.

After standing, I stacked the books in my arms and returned each one to its rightful place in the library. I returned to the center of the library, where the desks were, and raised my eyes to the writing curving over the archway separating me from the hall that led to the rest of the complex.

Et toto corde et pura mente invenies quod quaerere.

"The pure mind and heart will find what they seek," I translated out loud.

I needed to find a way back to that purity. Humble, unassuming, with no expectations of self. The library lived. It *breathed*. It would provide me with answers if I sought them with the proper mind and heart.

Closing my eyes, I blew out all the air in my lungs. I cleansed my mind of everything, even Mr. Smith, and focused solely on the chronicles. My mark ignited at the base of my skull, warming me with a familiar, calming sensation. The humming of the library started low, in the depths of my soul, and slowly rippled through me until it was all I heard and felt.

"Evolving blood seekers."

After I whispered the words, the hum focused on a single note, telling me the chronicles were ready to show me the answers I needed. I opened my eyes and allowed the library to guide me. One, two, three books… I followed the hum until I made my way back to my desk with eight books balanced in my arms.

Not knowing where to begin reading, I reminded myself of the power of the chronicles. I held my right hand out over the books until a slight vibration filled my palm. I giggled at the ticklish sensation, excited to discover a new superpower. Picking up the book, I opened the cover and dove into the narrative.

A story, woven together by different chroniclers across the generations in eight different books, formed in my mind. One that I wouldn't have found if I hadn't been looking for it. An ever-evolving type of demon let loose on Earth from the depths of hell, the blood seeker seemed to shift in abilities at various intervals in time. As I dug deeper into the chronicles, however, I found they were *regular* intervals. Every hundred and sixty-six years, to be exact.

And, when I calculated the timeframes, the blood seekers were due for another mutation.

This year.

I leaned back in my chair, my hand half-covering my mouth, as words and phrases from the chronicles spun through my head.

Faster. Quicker.

Strength is much greater in every known specimen that night stalkers have found in the past month.

Possible mutation to include an additional muscle in each leg.

The blood seeker tossed the night stalker at a distance greater than fifty metres.

Sight is far beyond the normal limits of any known living creature.

Hearing has increased to exceed that of a bat.

Connection between blood seekers seems to be strong, even to the point of communicating without speech.

Thought projection onto non-blood seekers might be possible.

Out of everything, the last entry hit me the hardest. If blood seekers could project thoughts onto others, could they also infiltrate dreams? And, if they could, were my dreams maybe not dreams at all, but something more sinister?

The idea nauseated me, not just because a blood seeker could have been in my dreams, but that Mr. Smith was in them, too. I remembered him referring to it as *his* dream, but maybe it had been a joint dream, one we shared. The things he said to me... my reaction to them. All of that could have been real. But, there was something much more fearsome looming over me.

Dark Man.

We couldn't take the chance on this mission. If Dark Man was real, if blood seekers were evolving once again, the mission couldn't move forward until we knew more. Until we could prepare for what came next. And, I had no idea how to prepare for any of it. Dream infiltration and possible mind control. Shared dreams between myself and Mr. Smith. Something strange was happening to all of us. Other than the small mentions in the chronicles, I needed Jia to reach out to the other chroniclers again, and with haste.

I jumped out of my chair and ran to the library exit, straight into Mr. Smith. I bounced off him and apologized. "I was just coming to see you."

"Did you find anything?" he asked.

"I did," I said, taking a few more steps away from him. My right hand swirled in the air, as if helping my mind conjure up what I had learned in the chronicles. "It's scattered information, but there is mention of changes to blood seekers. Mutation, evolution, whatever you want to call it, but they definitely have changed since we started keeping the chronicles."

He glanced at the books on my desk and blew out his breath. "What kind of changes?"

"Speed, senses. Things like that." I grimaced, not wanting to bring up the dream thing, but I couldn't hold back possibly important information. "There's a couple references to thought projection." Softly, I added, "Maybe even to dreams."

His gaze snapped to my face, but he didn't say anything. He didn't have to.

The need to distract him overcame me. I cleared my throat. "Strength, too," I said, my volume increasing. "In 1853, there was a tale of a blood seeker throwing a night stalker over fifty meters, however far that is." I shrugged, wondering if Mr. Smith was still focused on dreams. "It sounds like a long distance."

"It's over 160 feet," he said, looking to the floor.

"Good thing one of us knows math." I forced out a laugh, but the hollowness of it quickly faded once more to silence.

"What did it say about dreams?" he asked.

I scratched the back of my head and walked away, wishing I had some of Keira's Xanax to ease my anxiety. Back at my desk, I stacked the books to keep myself busy. "It's more a hypothesis than anything," I said, resisting the urge to run away. Did we really have to talk about this? If we had shared a dream—

He didn't ease up, walking until he stood beside me. "What's the hypothesis?"

"Thought projection," I said. "There's an idea that maybe they could project thoughts into dreams, too."

He shook his head. "That's impossible, though, unless it's with a companion."

His response caught me off-guard, and I looked at him. "What's a companion?"

"There are companions in lots of creature cultures. It's required for them to survive in our world. In the case of blood seekers, it's a mortal who shares their own blood with the blood seeker."

"People would let blood seekers... feed?" I shuddered, my stomach churning. "Off them?"

"It's rare, but it happens. Did the chronicles mention the thought projection occurring after a blood exchange?" Before I could ask what he meant, he said, "Where a human allows a blood seeker feed from them."

I rolled the stories through my mind. "No, they didn't. It's possible that other libraries have that information, though." Relief flowed through me. If an exchange of blood was required to project into a dream, then Dark Man hadn't infiltrated mine. I wasn't a companion for any blood seeker. Mr. Smith also wasn't one, so Dark Man couldn't have been in his dream, either.

"Let's have Jia contact the other complexes and find out what we can about this thought projection and the dreams thing."

"I agree," I said, "but we need to put off this mission. At least until we know what we're up against. The recon team said these blood seekers seem more evolved than what I'm finding in the chronicles, and—"

"We aren't delaying the mission. We have the nest tracked, we know the layout of the building. We can handle whatever comes our way."

My eyes narrowed, confused at his insistence to keep

going. "It's far too dangerous not knowing what—"

"I'm not concerned about that," he said, his tone firm, his decision final.

"Clearly. What about the others?"

"They'll be fine," he said. He started walking toward the library exit. "We've been on far harder missions than this."

I followed him to the small hallway leading to the main library door. "You're unbelievable. You really don't care about the rest of the team, do you?"

"You don't know—"

"Garrett, Keira, all the others. Doesn't matter who dies, so long as you feel you did everything you could to avenge Brent's death."

"You have no idea what you're talking about," he said. "That's the problem with you. Always thinking you understand this world. You've been here a few days. You have no right to judge me or my decisions."

"It's my job to give you all the information and make sure the survival rate is high, and you're ignoring that. This mission is too damn dangerous."

"It's already decided. We're going."

"You're risking everyone's life. For what? So you can feel better about not being there when Brent died? How the hell are you going to feel when *everyone* is dead? Or, is this just a suicide run for you? Brent's dead, so you may as well be, too?"

"Maybe when you lose someone, you'll get it."

I threw my hands up. "I just lost my entire family! For… for this! To be blindly led by you into a mission that's certain to fail!"

He stepped forward, towering over me. "You didn't lose *anyone*. They're still out there, breathing, talking, being alive."

My jaw tightened, and I spoke through clenched teeth. "If someone dies on this mission, that's on you. The only person *you* should be responsible for is yourself. You're leading them all into a possible death trap."

"That's ridiculous. Besides, if I died, then who would be around to save you?"

"I don't need saving." Trembling with rage, my fingers fused into fists at my sides, and my short fingernails dug crescent moons into my palms.

"What are you going to do? Kick all the blood seekers in the groin?" His condescending laugh rolled toward me.

My right fist swung wildly at his jaw. He caught it before it could connect, grabbed my left arm, and walked me backward until I hit the wall. Trapped, I struggled against his strong grip.

"Let me go," I said through clenched teeth, but my demand sounded weak in the face of his unbridled anger.

"How dare you," he said. "You come into our lives and just... You can't just..."

And, then I recognized it. Not anger. Not with me. Something else, something much more dangerous.

A soft yelp tried to escape me as his lips crashed against mine. Every second of our time together – all the bitterness, sarcasm, frustration, sadness – came out in that kiss. And, as much as I wanted it to end, I *needed* it to continue. As if physical separation would kill us both.

But, devolving under the weight of our emotions could also have the same effect.

His grip on me loosened, and I shoved him away as hard as I could, severing the kiss. "What the hell is wrong with you?" I shouted the question and stormed out of the library.

Chapter Twenty-five

I hopped into the first available elevator, grateful Mr. Smith didn't follow me. After opening the panel and pressing the button for the top floor, I slammed the side of my fist into the wall. Pain reverberated through my wrist and arm, and I shook my hand out, cursing Mr. Smith. The man was infuriating... but more than that... he was... was...

The doors to the elevator slid open, and I blindly wandered down the darkened hall to the balcony. My brain had collapsed on itself, quite possibly imploded in my skull, and I needed to relieve the pressure from whatever it was Mr. Smith was doing to me. He certainly had made my life much, much harder since we first met. Why did he have that aggravating, irritating, want-to-jump-off-the-nearest-cliff effect on me?

My hand and head both throbbed, but determination kept me going until I reached the balcony. Surely, he wouldn't chase me down. The last face I needed to see was his. I wished I could go the next year without running into him or even hearing his name.

Except, he oversaw the complex, and he was assigned to keep me safe during missions. Avoiding him, even for a day, would never work. Damn the luck.

Resting my hands on the balcony railing, I stared at the sun setting over the mountains, much as it had when Mr. Smith showed me the place. The scene calmed my jumping nerves and eased the tension in my muscles, and I focused solely on the hues cresting the nearest mountain.

Lights flickered on below me at ground level, just bright enough to show the way to the entrance of the complex. I imagined no one beyond the mountain could see them, and I briefly wondered how far I could get without a vehicle. Was it possible to escape my claustrophobic confines and make it back home? Hear my dad's voice call me "Magpie?" Listen to my mom bragging on Miller and Holly? Laugh with Liz over something stupid we did? What I wouldn't have given for just five minutes of my old life.

Movement in the shadows of the lights caught my attention. I squinted and could make out a shape, then several more. The scouting team had returned the night before and hadn't left the complex. Who could be—

Despite the great distance between the balcony and the dirt road, I could see one of the figures look up at me. I knew who it was before he stepped into the light.

Dark Man.

It wasn't possible. He wasn't real... he *couldn't* be real. I had to be dreaming again. I must have left the library, angry at Mr. Smith, and went to my room to fall asleep. Yes, that had to be it, because Dark Man didn't exist. He was only in my dreams, and I only dreamt of him because of the chronicles I'd buried myself in the past few days.

But, there he was, and there were others with him. I couldn't see him clearly, not in the traditional sense, but I *felt* him – and he felt me. The connection we had... there was no explanation for it. Yet, he was in my head. Again.

My consciousness floated away to someplace where it couldn't make rational decisions, and Dark Man filled the void. My eyes drifted closed, my mouth smiled... all beyond my will. Something inside of me needed to be next to him, to experience everything he had to teach me. My life at the complex was nothing compared to what it would be like with him. To reach that next level of evolution, power, *desire.*

His voice flooded my mind. *"Come with me, pet."*

My palms gripped the railing, and I leaned over it.
"It's not too far for us start our life together."
My resolve strengthened. I had to go to him. My foot planted itself in front of the railing while my opposite leg swung over the top of it. Once I had climbed over the rail, I turned around, the heels of my feet holding me up on the narrow ledge. I stared down at my destiny while gripping the iron behind me.

"It's time."

I let go of the railing.

Strong arms wrapped around me from behind, keeping me from falling. My mind jolted, as if I woke up, and I recognized the immediate danger. How did I get on the edge of the balcony?

"I've got you, Madison." Mr. Smith's voice provided little comfort as I faced down the distance between myself and the ground. The fire escape he helped me down from at my hotel looked like a baby step in comparison.

"Spencer?" My voice sounded so small, and my body trembled. "Don't… don't let me go."

"I won't," he said, "but we have to get you turned around."

My gaze still fixated on where Dark Man had stood a few moments earlier, I stuttered. "I… I can't. I can't do it."

"You can," he said. "I have faith in you. It's just a small turn, and then we'll get you back over to this side."

My breathing quickened to the point that I thought I would pass out. "I'm going to die, aren't I? I'm going to fall, and—"

"No, no, Madison. You won't. I promise. I won't let anything happen to you."

I wanted to believe him.

"We're going to do this slowly and together, okay? Just listen to my voice, and we'll get you through this."

I nodded, too afraid to speak in case it pushed me over the edge.

"One at a time, lift your feet and scoot them back so

you're on your tiptoes."

Starting with my right foot, I did as he instructed.

"Now, I need you to take one hand off the railing—"

"No! I can't let go!"

"Just one hand. You're going to pivot until you're facing me. I won't let you go."

Exhaustion nipped at the heels of adrenaline. If I didn't move soon, I knew I'd fall to my death. I loosened the grip of my left hand until it was free from the rail. I didn't fall. Mr. Smith had too strong of a hold on me. With his guidance, I raised my left foot and let it dangle over the edge as he helped me turn around to face the railing.

I had never been happier to see his face.

"You're almost there," he said, an encouraging smile crossing his lips. "Raise one leg and swing it over."

As soon as my leg straddled the railing, he tugged and lifted until I landed on the balcony, falling on my side. I didn't care about the possible scrapes or bruises. He helped me to my feet, and I gripped him in a tight embrace, afraid if I let go, I'd plummet over the side.

"What the hell, Madison?" he whispered in my ear.

"Dark Man," I said.

He released me and examined my wide eyes.

"Dark Man is real. I saw him." My memory returned in a flash, and shame crept across my face. "He told me… he said to jump."

"Who's Dark Man?"

"The blood seeker in my dreams."

Mr. Smith's face paled. I had forgotten he'd seen Dark Man in my dream – *our* dream. "I saw movement down there," he said, "but I didn't see anything specific."

"It was Dark Man and other blood seekers. I don't know how they found me here. I thought it was just… that *he* was just a dream."

Keira and Garrett rushed out onto the balcony before Mr. Smith could ask any other questions. "Mads!" Keira wrapped her arms around me. "Jiong said something was wrong on The

Ridge. He saw you on the cameras..." Letting me go, she asked, "Were you going to jump off the edge?"

"I wasn't..." But, that wasn't true. If Mr. Smith hadn't come in time, I would be a bloodied pancake on that poorly lit dirt road.

"We have a problem," Mr. Smith said. "I don't know how, but a blood seeker is projecting thoughts onto her. It's... it's in her dreams, too."

Garrett shook his head. "A blood seeker can't connect with a mortal unless they're a companion." He cast his gaze toward me. "You're not a companion, are you?"

"No, of course not!" My defiant answer came out harsher than I intended. "I mean, I would never let a blood seeker feed on me. If anyone wanted my blood, I never would have agreed to that."

"But, there had to be a blood exchange for anything like that to happen," Keira said. "If it were even possible at all, which..." She looked at Mr. Smith. "Is it even possible for a blood seeker to enter a human's dreams?"

"It must be," he said. "Madison found some reference to it in a chronicle."

"There was never a blood exch..." My face elongated, and my mouth parted. "Oh, no. It couldn't be that."

"What is it?" Mr. Smith asked.

"The night you rescued me from my hotel suite. I was talking to my parents on the phone. Mom said something stupid, and I cut my finger on a paring knife. I cleaned up the blood, though."

"Did you rinse off the wound first?" Keira asked. "Let the blood clot before bandaging it?"

"No, I just wrapped it in a paper towel," I said. "When it stopped bleeding, I threw that with the lemon in the trash... You don't think that—"

"Blood exchange," Garrett said. "Accidental, but it happened."

"Dark Man took my blood from the towel and lemon?" The thought revolted me, but it seemed the only explanation.

"They somehow knew you were the next chronicler, which is why they were after you," Keira said. "It makes sense that they'd want a direct line to your mind by taking in your blood, and if you immediately wrapped your finger in the towel without letting the blood clot first, they would have had enough for an exchange."

Silence permeated the air for several minutes, until Mr. Smith broke it. "They know where we are. We know where they are. And, they want Madison."

I dreaded his next words, but I knew they would be right.

"We can't delay this mission any longer," he said. "We leave tonight."

Chapter Twenty-six

"That's him." I pointed to the corner of the monitor, my heart racing at the image.

Jiong stopped the playback of the external camera footage. Other heads – Mr. Smith, Keira, Garrett, and Andre – all leaned forward, most of them squinting as they studied the screen.

"Do you see him?" I asked them, eagerness in my tone. Anything to validate I wasn't going crazy.

"I do see him," Mr. Smith said.

I exhaled with relief that someone else could see my personal demon.

"You call him Dark Man?" Mr. Smith asked me.

"He's got dark hair and dark, dead eyes. I didn't know what else to call him."

"When we scouted the nest, he was there," Andre said from beside me. "He definitely acted as the leader. At least he seemed more authoritative than the others. Jiong, can you move the frames forward? It looks like there is someone with him."

"I saw at least three others," I said, "but it was hard to tell."

The image on the monitor jumped forward, one frame at a time until another arm came into view. The owner of the arm's head dodged into view for a split second, and I instantly recognized him.

"That's Mullet Man," I said.

All eyes focused on me.

"He has this greasy, red mullet," I added. Another memory from my dream flashed through my mind. "And, a gold tooth."

"We saw him, too," Andre said. "He seems to be... Dark Man's right hand."

Silence fell on us for several long, uncomfortable moments before Mr. Smith spoke. "I need the room, guys."

I moved to file out with the others, but he grabbed my arm, stopping me.

"Not you," he said. His grip remained tight on my forearm until the door shut behind the leaving group. He let go of me, and I stepped away from him.

"What is it?" I asked, hoping he'd make our discussion quick.

Instead of answering, he sat on the edge of Jiong's desk, picked up the phone, and dialed. "Jia? It's Spencer. Cut all feed to this office." He paused before saying, "No, all feed. Audio and video." Another silence, then, "Thank you." He nestled the receiver in the cradle and shifted his attention back to me.

Cornered. I'd heard the phrase a thousand times before, but I'd never actually felt it until then. I was trapped with this man, who drove me insane on every level, and he had just cut off all ties to the outside world.

Maybe, he was going to kill me.

The thought, ridiculous as it was, bounced around my mind as my eyes darted around the room, searching for my escape. The door wasn't too far away from me, but I knew I'd never reach it in time. If I could somehow incapacitate him for—

"Do I scare you or something?" His question sent my heart into a race for its own exit from my frozen body.

"No," I said, not entirely convinced.

"I've never seen someone try to get away from me faster than you do," he said. "And, this isn't the first time."

"I... I, uh..." I had to come up with a quick explanation. "You told Jia to cut the video feed. I was looking for the cameras since I hadn't noticed any in here."

He hesitated, as if determining whether to believe me. "They're recessed in areas that they aren't easily found. It's hard for one person to monitor all operations. Having cameras and audio helps. The only places we don't have them are in the bedrooms."

Makes sense, I thought, but it didn't explain why he stopped the feed.

"I had a dream last night where I saw your 'Dark Man,'" he said, "but I have a feeling you already know that. You had the same dream, didn't you?"

"I don't know if it was the *exact* same dream—"

"You were there, we... had a conversation, then the blood seekers came."

"That sounds a little... familiar... maybe," I said, willing him to discuss any part of the dream other than our "conversation." The rest of it was bad enough.

"He could control you in the dream," Mr. Smith said. "Make you do whatever he wanted."

"But, the dreams can't be real."

"Dreams? There's been more than one?"

My eyes closed as I lowered my head. Why did I have to open my mouth? "Just the one last night and another one. I don't really want to talk about—"

"It's important," he said. "I think the dreams are real in that the players are real, but more than that. It's like we shared a dream, and we're both conscious of it today."

"Which is why it can't be real. I can understand him getting into my dreams now that we know he had access to my blood. But, you? That makes no sense."

"We're all bound together by our marks. Maybe it's possible that you... I don't know, willed me into the dream?"

A laugh barreled out of me, and I crossed my arms. "Well, I don't know how *that* would happen. Besides, you were only in one of the two dreams."

"I don't know, either. I'm guessing here. This is all very new for me." His shoulders heaved, and he let out a long breath. "I'm more concerned about his ability to control your actions. Is that what happened tonight? He controlled you to hop the railing and was trying to persuade you to jump?"

I lowered my head in shame. "Yes."

"Oh... damn, Madison. You could have died. Given this control he has over you, I should leave you here during this mission—"

"Then, leave me—"

"—but he knows where you are. I can't leave you unprotected. If you're here without protection, he could just come back and control your mind."

I silently agreed with Mr. Smith. If he hadn't stopped me from jumping, I'd be flattened against the dirt road right now. Dark Man could easily return and try it again, or command me to do much worse.

"Yet, if I take you with us, I don't know if you'll be able to stop yourself from being controlled again."

"I stopped him in the dream," I said. "He had complete control over me then, but I got out from under it. Maybe, I can do that again or block him somehow."

"You did, didn't you?" His squinted eyes inspected my face. "Just a thought, but without another blood exchange, his ability to control you should lessen. Before that happens, though, I need to know you can stop him if it comes to that. What was it that broke his control in the dream?"

I thought for a moment, then said, "Something he said about being infected. The virus. It made me come to when I realized I didn't want to be like him." I swallowed against my words, but they came out anyway. "I used to be afraid of dying, but now I know that's not the worst thing out there. I don't want to become a blood seeker."

Mr. Smith scooted off the edge of the desk. "You won't become one," he said. "I won't let that happen."

"If it does, if this mission goes sideways and he controls me or whatever, promise me you'll kill me instead of letting me become like him."

"You won't—"

"Just, promise me. Please."

My words hung in the thick air between us, unable to move with the tension holding them hostage. I needed his promise so much more than he understood. I could never become like one of them, especially not under the control of Dark Man. Killing innocents, like my family or Liz. Drinking their blood to survive. And, that *smell*...

"I—"

A knock on the door interrupted Mr. Smith, and his tightened facial muscles relaxed. He walked past me and opened the door.

"Are you guys ready?" Garrett asked from behind me.

I turned around and nodded at him. "We don't have much of a choice, do we?" My voice cracked. "I really screwed this up for—"

"You didn't do anything wrong," Mr. Smith said.

Garrett vocalized agreement beside him. "There's no way any of us could have known that they would use your blood to get to you. And, you had no idea what was after you or that your blood could be a gateway."

But, it was too late for them to take away my guilt. "Brent lost his life, I got called up, and now I've led the blood seekers who killed him straight to you and—"

"Stop," Mr. Smith said, his palms gripping my upper arms. "You can't blame—"

"If someone dies on this mission, it's my fault," I said.

"No," Garrett said. "We don't shell out blame here at the complex. Even if we did, none of this is your fault. Just listen to Spence. I'll gather the team and meet you guys in the loading bay." He turned to go, but stopped. "Um, Keira left you some clothes for the mission on your bed," he said to me. He exited the room, leaving the door cracked open behind him.

With my gaze fixed on Mr. Smith, I whispered, "I'm sorry. I'm really scared right now."

"I know, and it's normal. Close your eyes and let your

mark take over. Let it calm you."

I did as he said and focused my thoughts on the mark. I welcomed the rush through my veins, then realized my newfound relaxation didn't just come from the mark, but from Mr. Smith's proximity. One of the many effects he had on me.

My eyes popped open, and I stepped away from him. "I'm good," I said, holding up my hands to put space between us.

I caught a quick glimpse of his smile before he opened the door and led the way out.

Chapter Twenty-seven

I looked like a cat burglar, if anyone still called it that. My mom had always used that phrase, and it stuck somewhere in the back of my mind. Not that I'd ever seen a cat burglar, but what I saw in the mirror must have resembled one.

Heading for the door to my room, I adjusted the long, black sleeves of my tight shirt, then tugged it down, over the waist of stretchy, black jeans. At least we didn't have to wear pants or stiff jeans. Much too uncomfortable for a mission.

Music pounded through the wall my bedroom shared with Mr. Smith's. It had just started, making me curious as to why he wasn't ready to leave yet. Had something changed in the mission?

I exited my room and followed the sound of the heavy guitar and pounding bass until I reached his door. I rapped on the wood, my knuckles hitting the door as hard as possible so he could hear me. After a few seconds, I repeated the knock. I almost gave up when his door swung open.

"Yeah?" he asked, standing in black jeans with no shirt. Again. "Are you ready to go?"

"I am, but I heard the music."

"Sorry about that," he said, rushing back into his room. He turned down the volume on the speakers attached to a computer on a corner desk.

Stepping over the threshold, I watched him scurry back to

his bed and grab the shirt laid out across it. After he pulled the shirt over his head, he said, "I always listen to music before and on the way for a mission. Kinda puts me in the right mood."

"It's okay," I said. "I don't mind it, in case you were wondering."

"Not too loud for you?"

I smirked and said, "Never seems to be loud enough."

A surprised smile crossed his lips, and he nodded. "Okay. Okay then." He went to his closet, disappeared for a moment, and came out with a black shoulder holster without any guns.

"Do guns work on blood seekers?" I asked, remembering the machete he carried at my hotel suite.

"Not to kill, but they can slow them down." He slipped into the holster. "I had this modified so my machete fits on my back." From his bed, he grabbed his machete and locked it into place.

"Do I get a weapon of some sort?"

"We never had time to practice with a machete. I suppose we can give you a gun, but without any experience—"

"I come from a small town in Kansas," I said. "Grew up hunting and fishing. Got my first buck at seventeen."

"Are you *sure* you're a romance writer?" he asked.

"These aren't exactly the kinds of things that I talk about in interviews. Liz always tells me – I mean, *told* me that I needed to show a softer side for the readers."

"How are you with handguns?"

"Better than I am with a rifle."

"We'll head down to the armory and get you geared up. You can decide which one works best for you." He paused for a moment, then asked, "Can I make a small suggestion? Your hair. Don't leave it loose like it is. You don't want to give anyone anything they can grab."

The little things I would never have thought of, like the necessity for hair to be pulled back completely, raised my incompetence level in my already doubtful mind. Despite the mark telling me where I belonged, I couldn't fathom how I would manage this world. My life expectancy seemed much shorter than the others in the complex.

As we walked out of his room and toward the elevators, I redid my ponytail in favor of a tight bun. At the end of the hall, just beyond the last elevator, Mr. Smith pulled out a set of keys from his jeans and unlocked a door, one I had seen before, but to which I'd never paid much attention. Down the short hall was another elevator with only a "down" arrow on the wall. The surprises of the complex never ceased.

My thoughts wandered across any other details of Dark Man knowing my identity, searching for anything I may have missed. Stepping into the elevator behind Mr. Smith, I instantly landed on an alarming one.

"They know who I am and where I am," I said. "What about my family? Friends? Are they safe?"

"They're fine."

A bit of panic tinged my voice. "How do you know?"

"Because the blood seekers, and this Dark Man… they know who you are. They knew before we did. If they were going to do something to your family or friends, they would have done it long before now." He fidgeted with his keys, moving each one from left to right over the top of the ring. "I, uh… I also have a few night stalkers from another complex watching them, and as of three hours ago, your family and closest friends were all unharmed."

"What?" My heart stopped, and my breath caught in my throat. He'd had my friends and family – the last semblances of my old life, not to mention, the people I loved the most – under surveillance and failed to mention it. I don't think I could have hated him more than in that moment.

Somehow, I restrained myself from killing him. "You've had people watching them? This whole time? Why didn't you tell me?"

"Because, somehow, I knew this is how you'd react."

His arrogant assumptions! Part of me reasoned that his motives for not telling me were much more than my angry reaction. That I would want to know all about their every activity. That I would succumb to homesickness instead of focusing on my work at the complex. That I would wallow in depression over not being able to see when others watched them every day.

But, it was much easier to blame him. To take my rage out on him. To let out all those emotions I'd suppressed about losing my family and turn him into a supervillain.

"How dare you keep this from me!" Fury over his deception clashed with renewed mourning over the loss of my family, and my body shook until it threatened to shatter into millions of pieces. "How long have you had people following them?"

"It doesn't matter how—"

"How long?" Threads of anger spun in my veins, and my rising blood pressure pounded in my head.

He lowered his voice and said, "Since the day we met in New York."

I huffed, but he spoke first.

"The blood seekers knew who you were before we did. I figured once we got to you, they might go after your family to bring you out of hiding."

The elevator alarm sounded, and I jumped back, hitting the wall. Looking at the two buttons on the wall, both without markings, I realized neither of us had pushed one. I jabbed the bottom one, hitting it several times, even after it lit up.

When the elevator jolted to life, I said, "You *lied* to me. You said my family was safe."

"I needed you to be mentally present to do your job. You can't focus on all the other stuff you left behind."

"That 'other stuff' are people I care about."

"They are your past."

"No, no, they're not," I said. "Everyone keeps saying that, but they're *not* my past."

"They have to be. If you want to survive for long in this world, you have to stop thinking of them as your family."

"But—"

He stepped forward and placed his hands on my shoulders. "I get that it's hard, but it's the only way. You need to remember that you're not in this life for no reason at all. We save *lives*. Thousands upon thousands of people survived an encounter with a monster because of us. Thousands upon thousands more were never attacked because we terminated the threat. Those lives include your past family and friends."

I closed my eyes and air shuddered through my lungs. As much as it hurt, there was no arguing with anything he said.

"We will eradicate this nest of blood seekers," he continued after my eyelids cracked open. "That means eliminating any threat to those you care about. But, I need you in the game. Here, now. With us."

Something sparked in those blue eyes with his words, knowledge that this mission was only partly about revenge for his brother's death. The rest of it had to do with me. Taking care of the blood seekers who could hurt me and my family – my *past* family. Maybe he and I both realized it at the same time, but his motive for going after them wasn't entirely selfish.

But, to do that, to assist with this mission and get out alive, I also had to relinquish my fears, anger, and the sense of betrayal – that *he*, of all people, had betrayed me. Yet, beyond all logic, my trust in him didn't waver.

"I'm here," I said as the elevator doors opened, "and I'm ready to do this."

Chapter Twenty-eight

If my dad and brother could have seen the armory at the complex, they'd think they'd gone to good ol' boy huntin' heaven.

The sheer number of guns on the walls, all arranged by caliber and type, made the Midwest girl in me drool a bit. A snub-nosed Taurus Mini Revolver caught my attention and drew me to it as if it were the only weapon in the room. I removed it from the hooks on the wall and grinned at my new shiny object.

"That's only got five shots in it," Mr. Smith said.

"That's all I need." Glancing in his direction, I added, "You're supposed to carry the big guns and the machete. This is a 'just in case' measure." Looking back at the gun, I said, "She shore is purty," emphasizing a hick accent in my speech.

"Then, she's all yours."

"Miller would be so jealous right now," I said, wishing I could share my find with my brother.

I turned around, and a glint from a case across the room caught my attention. I wandered over, my fingers caressing the glass covering the cache of knives, ones like I'd never seen. Latin engraved on some of the blades, Enochian on others, and a mix of Hebrew and Greek on one particular silver dagger in the center of all the others. Wonderment filled my mind as it raced with the translations.

Over my shoulder, Mr. Smith said, "They're beautiful, aren't they?"

"Stunning," I said, breathless from his closeness. How could I go from being so angry with the man to thinking about him in ways that drove me insane? In just minutes, my emotions had flipped again, although part of me still wanted to murder him.

I moved forward and walked to the right, down to another case of knives. "So many different inscriptions on these."

"For every creature we battle, there's a different means of destruction. Let's just say that we have a lot of cool toys here."

"I can't believe you grew up around all this. My childhood seems so mundane now."

"It's not the easiest life," he said.

"So I'm learning."

"There are holsters over there"—he gestured toward a cabinet in the back right corner— "and you'll need something for close combat."

"Um… I don't plan on getting close enough for combat."

He exhaled in exasperation, but smiled all the same. "Humor me on this one, okay?" He opened another closed steel cabinet. Daggers and knives all shapes, sizes, and deadliness hung, just waiting for use. Pulling one of the shorter daggers off the wall, he said, "This one should work. It's similar to the one I used on my first mission."

"Oh." I accepted the blade. "I'm getting weapons from the kiddie menu, I see." Before he could respond to my sarcasm, I said, "Thank you, though. I am great with guns, not so much with knives and all that, so the starter pack is probably best." I realized he hadn't picked out any weapons for himself. "Aren't you going to get something?"

"I tend to stick with what I know. My machete is an all-occasion, non-discriminatory weapon that's served me well for the past ten years."

"Then, I say let's not jinx it."

"That's the plan." He led me out of the armory and further down the hallway. "I…" He cleared his throat. "I also want to make sure we're good before we do this thing."

"Oh, uh... uh, yeah. We're fine."

"I mean, earlier... you know. I didn't—"

"We're good," I said, not wanting to dredge up the whole kissing or shared dream mess. Our relationship – or lack thereof – was complicated enough. "We have nothing to talk about."

"Good," he said, with what sounded like a tinge of disappointment in his tone. "Just wanted us both to go into this clear-headed."

I put on my best fake smile and said, "I've never been clearer."

"Me, too."

The problem was, I'd never been less clear about anything. My new life, the chronicles, going on a suicide mission, Mr. Smith and his irritating way of getting under my skin just so. None of it could be defined as "clear."

But, the mission had to move forward.

We stopped at steel double doors. "These lead to the loading bays. All our vehicles are in here, and it's the only way out of the complex."

My anxiety decided to make itself known, throwing my thoughts into further chaos. As if it weren't real before, I now recognized my own mortality. The world's largest and loudest stopwatch ticked away, counting down to my inevitable demise. Instinct told me to run. Logic told me I had no choice but to fight. Dark Man would keep coming. He'd already proven his confidence in walking straight up to the entrance of the complex. What was next? Strolling in for a hello and a bite to eat?

As if reading my mind, Mr. Smith said, "We have several other sets of impenetrable doors in the bays. No one can get in here, no matter how hard they try."

He opened the door on the right, and we walked into a room as large as an airport hangar. The immense size of the complex not lost on me, I wondered what else the inside of this mountain held that I had yet to see. The rest of the team waited for us, all decked out in their own cat burglar costumes, carrying various weapons. As if I didn't already comprehend the gravity of the mission, the somberness of the group penetrated my core. No one smiled, not even Keira or the always-cheerful Garrett.

I took my place amongst the others, who had all turned to look at Mr. Smith, their leader. *Our* leader.

"You all have your assignments," he said, "but given tonight's events, I'm having Andre stay with me to watch Madison."

Embarrassment flushed my face. Oh, the trouble I had caused since even before I arrived at the complex.

"We have five night stalkers from our East Coast complex who are already on their way," Mr. Smith continued. "They should arrive just before us. That's all they could spare." Turning to the left side of our group, he said, "Jia, Jiong, and Sandra are monitoring communications tonight."

I looked over to see all the non-night stalkers, the members of The Order, standing together. I recognized most of them, but there were a few new faces.

Mr. Smith bowed his head and closed his eyes. Around me, the others did the same as they spoke in unison. "*Sit aeterna Dei nobis et custodies in nostrorum curso malum.*"

My mind translated the Latin: "May the eternal God guide us and keep us in our quest against evil."

"Let's get those blood seeker heads rolling," Morgan said as an ending to the prayer.

The mood of the room shifted. The others around me laughed, whooped, and called out their "Amens."

"For Brent," Garrett said above the voices, which quickly echoed him.

"And, for Mads," Andre added. He winked at me as I glanced at him and flinched. "Not gonna let Dark Man get to her."

"For Mads," the group called out, including Mr. Smith.

As everyone disbursed in small groups and headed toward different vehicles, Mr. Smith came over to me. His hand slipped around my upper arm, and I walked with him. "From this moment on, you are with me," he said. "You don't leave me, not even by a few inches. If I'm killing a blood seeker, you step back, but only a little." We stopped at a black SUV, and he faced me, his hand still holding my arm. "Do you understand me?"

"I promise," I said. "I won't hesitate like at the hotel."

He stared at me for a moment, as if analyzing my answer for truthfulness, then said, "Just like everything else in the world, the first time is the hardest. This will get easier for you."

I let out a shaky breath, as if his words gave me permission to relax slightly. "Thank you."

He nodded and opened the back driver's side door to the SUV. I climbed in, and he followed. Andre entered the driver's seat, while Morgan jumped into the passenger seat. Doors slammed shut, seatbelts clicked. The engine revved to life, and the vehicle followed the others out of the bay, through a tunnel with minimal running lights, and onto the dirt road in the back of the complex.

Morgan twisted her head to look at Mr. Smith. "The usual playlist?"

"You know it," he answered. "It seems our new chronicler likes the heavier music."

Morgan grinned at me. "You're gonna get along just fine here." She depressed the button to turn on the radio, then swiveled the knob to the right, raising the volume.

Mr. Smith's hand brushed against my shoulder in a comforting gesture, then retreated. I glanced at him, expecting him to speak, but he only smiled. The corner of my mouth lifted, then I turned to look out the window as we exited the complex. Maybe we had more to talk about than either of us wanted to admit. But, until then, I focused my thoughts on surviving the mission and following his every instruction. If one or both of us didn't make it, nothing else would matter.

Chapter Twenty-nine

Despite having Mr. Smith at my side, Andre looming behind me, and my hand gripping my revolver, terror consumed me. I kept my anxiety hidden the best I could and refused to voice any concerns, no matter how many popped into my mind. Like Mr. Smith had warned me, I believed the blood seekers could smell my fear. The same as I could smell them.

Though the time neared three in the morning and it was mostly black outside, a few of the streetlights still working outside the factory shone a bit of light into the abandoned space. A graveyard of dilapidated conveyer belts and defunct machinery surrounded us. Particles of dust from the aged objects scattered through the beams of light, sparkling like specks of gold and rousing my allergies. My thumb and index finger of my left hand covered my nose just in case. Sneezing while sneaking through a factory and searching out blood seekers would be the pinnacle of my short career as a chronicler. If I survived, which was still doubtful, Mr. Smith would have one or fifty things to say about that later.

Other teams had approached the factory from different directions than us, covering the perimeter, breaching the building and flanking the enemy, or something like that, according to Mr. Smith. Yet, when I spied Keira, Morgan, and Colin's team of three nearing our left side, I realized that the usual strategy, as Mr. Smith called it, wasn't going as planned. Either we were in the wrong place, or the blood seekers hadn't stayed for the party.

Dread pulled my stomach to the floor, and my heart jumped into my throat. The odor of the blood seekers seemed much too strong for a long-ago nest vacated. No, they had been in the factory no more than an hour before we arrived.

Mr. Smith raised a hand in one of the rays of light, and the two teams I could see halted at the same time we did. Though shadows crossed his face, I could see his gaze exploring the area, carefully, deliberately, no doubt planning our next move. His machete to his side, he raised it slightly, as if expecting a blood seeker to jump out at any moment.

But, nothing moved.

My tense shoulders dropped despite the rest of my overly sore muscles remaining contracted. The adrenaline that had controlled my breathing since we arrived at the factory slowly eased out of my body, leaving behind fatigue. My eyelids drooped, just a bit at first, and exhaustion claimed me. My grip on the gun loosened. I could have fallen asleep on my feet, but something tethered me to the waking world. A tugging, a pulling, and then a voice.

"Madison!" Mr. Smith spoke my name in a loud whisper with a harsh, almost hissing tone.

I shook my head awake, and my eyes popped open. Mr. Smith grasped my forearm, and the intense expression on his face frightened me. A few seconds passed before I realized where we were. What we were doing. How could I sleep standing up in the middle of a mission—

The overwhelming stench racked my senses, and my eyes grew as the tension grabbed me once more. We were no longer alone in the factory.

And, we were surrounded.

Mr. Smith seemed to realize it when I did, but it was too late. Blood seekers crept out of every corner of the factory, using our tactical plan against us. Lights flickered on, no longer affording us the cover of darkness to silently kill our prey.

Several blood seekers ushered in the two teams we had left outside to monitor the situation and back us up.

As soon as I saw *him*, I understood what had happened to me. Why I had dozed off – if I could call it that. More like fell under his trance, the same one he could impose on me in my dreams. Mr. Smith had pulled me out of it, just like he had in the dream we shared. I did not know if I could withstand any more of his control.

I realized we were in the exact center of the factory floor. Dark Man stood in the doorway of where we had entered, Mullet Man to his left, and three other blood seekers around him. Without releasing my stare into Dark Man's dead eyes, I stepped back three paces, maybe four. In my peripheral, Andre moved up to Mr. Smith's right, his own machete poised for action.

"You can all put down your weapons." Dark Man's voice boomed throughout the space, echoing off bad acoustics.

I looked at Mr. Smith, wondering what we should do. My hand started to lower my gun toward the floor, but the side of Mr. Smith's face I could see remained hard. Stubborn. Driven. We wouldn't relinquish our weapons anytime soon.

"That's not going to happen," Mr. Smith said. "Even if you have guns, you won't shoot us. Your nest looks a bit hungry, which means they have to get closer to us to get their breakfast." His head twitched, and he smirked. "Most important meal of the day, isn't it?"

My lips parted, a bit shocked at his sarcastic response, but I figured I would have said something similar. He and I were so alike. Made me loathe him even more.

"You're right, of course," Dark Man said. "We will feast on you all." His eyes shifted toward me. "Except our little chronicler. My new *pet*."

With heavy breaths, I side-stepped until I stood behind Mr. Smith for protection.

"You'll do nothing to her," Mr. Smith said.

Dark Man huffed. "And, you'll be the first one she feeds from, Night Stalker."

Tapping on my outer thigh caught my attention. I glanced down, then immediately up so as not to give anything away. Mr. Smith's index finger knocked lightly against my leg, not randomly as I first thought, but in Morse code. He was signaling the other night stalkers. My eyes roamed toward Andre, and I saw him doing the same thing on the back of his thigh. For a second, I wondered why Mr. Smith used my leg, then quickly realized he had to, as I wouldn't be able to see the code from where I stood.

Dark Man continued speaking, but I tuned him out in favor of the Morse code. My brain logged and deciphered the taps — apparently my translation superpower wasn't limited to spoken languages, but also worked on codes.

Wait for my signal.

The same sentence repeated two more times before ceasing. My mind flooded with dozens of possibilities of what that signal might be. I told myself to stop overanalyzing and wildly predicting, and exhibit some patience. I would recognize it when it happened, so long as I trusted Mr. Smith. With him, it always seemed to come down to trust, no matter how reluctantly I gave it.

As if a wave from the ocean crashed into me, I wavered on my feet as water rippled across my brain, drowning and hypnotizing me. My equilibrium failed, and I faltered, tripping to the side, but not falling.

Dark Man's voice sounded in my mind as he beckoned me to come forward, to leave the safety of Mr. Smith and follow *him* instead. Whispered promises caressed me, but I fought him with every bit of strength I had left.

I rocked into the back of Mr. Smith's left shoulder.

He caught my arm and steadied me. "What's wrong, Madison?" he whispered.

His touch and voice brought lucidity to my mind once more. "Dark Man is trying to control me again," I said.

"Fight it," Mr. Smith said. "You're stronger than that. I've seen it."

I *was* stronger than Dark Man. I could defend my senses

against him, keep him out of my head. But, I needed a weapon to use. Something much more powerful than a revolver and a knife.

"You've been in my brain," I said to Dark Man. "But, I've been in yours, too."

"It doesn't work that way," he said.

"Yes, it does. The blood exchange works both ways," I continued, speaking much louder to grab his attention. With everyone focused on me, I said, "I know where each member of your nest is at right now and what they plan to do. I know your strategies, your tactics. There's *nothing* you can keep secret from me."

His facial muscles tightened, and unspoken threats floated in his dark eyes. "That's impossible," he said. "You're bluffing."

I *was* bluffing, but I couldn't let him know that. We had to somehow gain the upper hand in the standoff. "*De daemonium exolvuntur,*" I hissed in Dark Man's direction, just loud enough for him to hear. My mind called up the words I'd read in the chronicles, and it seemed to impact him. "You're in the middle of evolving again, just like you do every hundred and sixty-six years."

Dark Man quickly covered up his surprised expression by hardening it again. "How do you know that?"

"I told you. *Sanguinem commutationem.* Blood exchange. What else do you think I learned from you all those times you tried to get into my head and control me?"

"Interesting," Dark Man said.

A long pause followed, and I prayed for Mr. Smith's signal. I didn't know how much longer I could continue the farce.

"You are a feisty chronicler, aren't you?" Dark Man laughed. "Coming into your first nest, lying about getting into my head, putting all of your little night stalker friends at risk. I rather like that about you."

"I'm not ly—"

"If you knew everything I knew," Dark Man said, "if you were truly in my mind due to the blood exchange, then this won't surprise you at all." He held up his hand and wiggled his index finger.

My heart bounced in my chest as its beating spread out of control. *Did I just get everyone killed?*

A blood seeker I hadn't yet seen emerged from the shadows and took his place next to Dark Man. My jaw slacked and eyes widened as recognition came over me.

Dark Man had called my bluff, and he had won.

I stared at the new blood seeker's dark brown hair, a good inch below shoulder-length, tousled, and in need of a trim. His familiar blue eyes seemed colder than even Dark Man's. Though clean-shaven (did the dead blood seekers even grow hair?) and a few inches taller, he looked just like Mr. Smith. As he crossed his arms, I didn't need a picture, didn't need a description or introduction, to know who this was standing in front of us.

Brent Frye. Mr. Smith's younger brother and our former chronicler.

Chapter Thirty

My mind flashed with a thousand thoughts at once. Brent had fallen on the previous mission, but they hadn't been able to retrieve his body – commonplace, according to Mr. Smith. But, he hadn't died, not in the traditional sense. He had been infected with the virus. Even with the team monitoring the nest, the other blood seekers must have kept him hidden from view so that no one from our side would know the truth about Brent's fate.

The emotion radiating from Mr. Smith encompassed me in its bubble of pain. Betrayal. Not a purposeful traitor, but one nonetheless. Yet, there was more suppressing his usual strength. Sadness, but beyond that, defeat. The leader of our complex's always-hardened shell had cracked.

My neck rotated as my gaze traveled between each group of night stalkers. Keira, Garrett, Morgan, Harvey, Colin, Andre, Rich, Brady… plus five new night stalker faces from the other complex. All of their expressions varied, but they settled around the same crushing thought that permeated the group. Brent was alive, yet dead. And, he was standing on the wrong side of the fight.

"Good to see you, *brother*," Brent said.

"I wish I could say the same," Mr. Smith said. "What happened to you?"

"What happened?" An incredulous laugh played on his

words. "What happened is this incompetent bunch of night stalkers couldn't wait two minutes to confirm if I was dead or alive. Sure, I was down and in a bad way, but I wasn't *gone*. Not until after they left."

"Brent—"

"And, where were you, the almighty Spencer? Off on some other, more important mission. Too busy to protect your baby brother, the chronicler. But, I can see you have a new one already to watch over. Of course, you're going to let her down, just like you did me. Soon enough, she'll be one of us."

I cringed behind Mr. Smith, my fists bunching up the back of his shirt, afraid to look at his brother or Dark Man any longer.

"Don't hide, Chronicler," Brent said. "He can't save you. Besides, it's far better on this side. And, from what I understand, you enjoy the blood just a little more than a human should."

As my face flushed, I could sense the questions — and possible judgement — from the other night stalkers. No one knew of my dreams except Mr. Smith, and he was only present for the second one. The first one, the more disturbing of the two, I had kept secret.

But, Dark Man knew about it.

Lost in my own personal panic, I didn't see Mr. Smith's signal or the start of the battle. I have no idea who attacked first or from which direction it started, but begin it did. Two blood seekers charged Mr. Smith, but he quickly dispatched them with Andre's help. The sounds of an epic fight surrounded me, all while I stood paralyzed between Mr. Smith and Andre.

A gunshot echoed through the factory, followed by a scream filled with pain. I twisted my head in time to see Rich fall victim to a feasting blood seeker. Another blood seeker pounced on Rich's flopping body, and bones crunched as the blood flew. Morgan raced to his aid and beheaded both, but it was too late for Rich.

Mr. Smith grabbed my arm and dragged me across the

room. He hissed at me to get out my gun, which I did. I held it close to my chest and rotated to make sure there were no oncoming blood seekers. Mr. Smith ushered me to a corner of the room, saying something about it being safer for me. I simply nodded, my overwhelming ineptitude shining through. How could anyone ever get used to this... chaos?

I breathed through my fear and talked my frozen limbs into moving. Standing there, I'd never survive. Though Mr. Smith hovered near me, killing one blood seeker after another, I had to protect myself if needed. Dark Man's presence doused me in terror once more, and I knew he inched closer to me. The strongest of all the blood seekers, I didn't know how Mr. Smith could kill him as easily as some of the weaker ones. And, then, there was the matter of Brent.

Three blood seekers charged Mr. Smith, drawing him further away from me as he fought. I held out my gun, pointing it at nothing, but ready for anything. My brain cursed my sedentary lifestyle, and questions fired at will. Why hadn't I been more active and in shape? Why couldn't I have had more time to train before this mission? Why couldn't I be braver, like Keira? And, why the hell did blood seekers have to smell so damned awful?

A gleaming gold tooth appeared in my view, and my body decided to go into shock as Mullet Man came closer to me. The gun shook in my hands, but somehow, I managed to squeeze off a shot. The bullet slammed into Mullet Man's shoulder, jerking him back. Only for a second. He regained his stance, and his smile grew.

"I've heard how good you taste," he said, his blood teeth descending. "I can't wait to try you myself."

I squeezed the trigger again, but he hit my arm a split second before, causing the gun to point up as it fired. He threw me to the ground and wrenched my neck to the side. He pulled down the collar of my shirt, exposing my skin. I screamed for Mr. Smith, but Mullet Man's teeth still penetrated just above my shoulder. Excruciating pain shot through my body, involuntary tears raced down my cheeks, and for the first time,

I understood what it was like to want to die. To crave death more than anything else. To need it desperately… just so the agony would cease.

Mullet Man lifted off me, and through my tears, I saw Mr. Smith throw him down to the ground. As Mullet Man tried to stand, Mr. Smith's machete seared through his neck, severing his head.

Though grateful for the intervention, I couldn't move. Nothing in my body seemed to function, except my eyes.

Mr. Smith knelt in front of me, and his hands pressed down on my wound, his gaze meeting mine. "No, Madison. No, no, no. You have to stay here with me."

I wanted to respond, my mouth attempted to move, but nothing happened. I couldn't communicate with him, couldn't stand, couldn't run away to safety.

"Madison, I need you to hang in there," he said. "You can't leave me now."

Dull panic swarmed my mind as I watched Brent step up behind him. I tried to signal with my eyes, but it didn't work. Brent pulled Mr. Smith up and threw him against some machinery. My gun rested beside me, but my hand wouldn't move to grab it and shoot Brent.

Another form filled my vision, eclipsing the fight between Mr. Smith and Brent, and I knew who it was before he lowered himself to my level. Dark Man. I needed to do something, fight back somehow, but my body seemed disconnected from my brain.

"You're wondering what's happening to you," he said, his soothing voice washing over me. "Like some predators, when we bite, we release a paralytic. Makes our prey a little easier to control. Although I wanted to have you first, I'm glad someone else prepped you for me."

I grunted, but no words came out.

He turned my body to the side and slid his arms under me. Lifting me up, he said, "Let's go somewhere a little quieter. How does that sound, pet? Some alone time?"

As he walked, I captured the sight of Mr. Smith battling

his brother. I could hear the other night stalkers fighting, and I prayed the rest of them were still alive. Dark Man carried me across the factory floor, and I wondered how anyone would find me if he managed to abscond with me.

They won't find you, I thought. *You're going to end up like Brent. Dead but alive with an insatiable thirst for blood and a more-than-unpleasant odor.*

The night seemed much darker than it had when we first arrived, but my numb flesh could no longer feel the chill of the air. A door opened to a vehicle, and Dark Man slipped me onto the backseat. He climbed in beside me and laid my head down on his lap. Brushing stray hairs away from my face, he gave directions to the unseen driver. The car engine roared to life, and soon, the factory and Mr. Smith were far behind.

Chapter Thirty-one

Rays of sunlight broke through a small opening in the thick layer of gray clouds as the car pulled up to our destination. Once upon a time, as a child, hopeful and innocent, I could name every type of cloud. These were just ugly. Filled with the promise of gloom and possibly a bleak storm later.

In and out of consciousness throughout our drive, the journey blurred in my mind. Where we were, how far we traveled, there was no way for me to tell. The numbness in my body had tapered off at some point, but the effects of the paralytic still restricted my limbs to a degree. I could lift an arm, but only a few inches. My leg itched, but I couldn't reach it to relieve the nuisance.

When the car engine died down, Dark Man helped me out of the vehicle by lifting me into his strong arms. A large, blue home with white shutters lingered in front of us, and as far as I could turn my head, I didn't see any other signs of life. Dark Man carried me into the house, much like an eager groom entering the honeymoon suite.

As we moved through hallways, various blood seekers flitted in and out of my view. Up two flights of stairs, past more curious blood seekers, the house never seemed to end. Eventually, we ended up in a bedroom, where he laid me down on a comfortable bed. Still groggy from Mullet Man's bite, I couldn't see much else in the room outside of my captor.

Dark Man's fingers combed through my hair, and I realized at some point he must have taken it out of the tight bun.

"I know you're tired, pet," he said, lovingly running his fingertips across my cheek. "You'll be able to sleep soon enough, but the next few days will be… delightfully agonizing for you. But, once you're through the worst of the pain, you will change into something you've never dreamed of. The power and strength alone. There's no comparison."

My mouth moved to protest, to beg for mercy, but words failed me.

"Don't be scared," he said. "It's a beautiful transition into a higher evolution. Into what we are meant to become."

"No," I managed to get out before exhaustion took over again.

"Let's get this off you." He shimmied my shirt out from under me and raised my head to pull it off, leaving me in only a bra and jeans. "That's better." He moved my head to the side until my wound was exposed. A finger pressed into the bite, sending pain through my nerves into every part of my body. "Just like I thought," he said. "Dry. Time to fix that."

Out of the corner of my eyes, I watched his blood teeth descend, just as Mullet Man's had before he struck. Within seconds, Dark Man's teeth punctured my skin. A barely audible scream escaped me, but there was no way to fight him. The paralytic entered my body, rendering me helpless. The only feeling left in me was the gentle sucking of my lifeblood.

As my head swarmed in a sea of dizziness, Dark Man lifted off from me. "The virus is inside you now," he said. The back of his hand caressed my cheek, a lover's touch in a most frightful form. "You'll need to feed soon, but for now, just sleep."

My stomach revolted at the sight of my blood smeared across his mouth, and my spirit gave one final push for a fight, but I couldn't move. Not when his lips touched mine, not when he engaged me in a one-sided kiss. The metallic taste of him – of *me* on him – pushed me over the edge, and I blacked out.

When I regained consciousness, Dark Man was no longer on the bed with me. Other voices, two men and a woman, had joined him in the room in faint conversation. My eyes fluttered open, and I tried to raise my head. When my neck didn't cooperate, I lulled my head to the side to try to catch a glimpse of them, but they merged into blurry figures. I let my eyelids fall shut again and instead tried to focus on their hushed voices.

"You prepared the blood?" Dark Man asked.

"Precisely how you asked," one of the men said.

"Here it is," the woman said. "May I inquire—"

"You will be rewarded for your patience," Dark Man said, "as soon as the chronicler is one of us. For now, your job is to provide her the blood she needs."

Heavy footsteps approached the bed, and I forced my eyes back open. The mattress dimpled with Dark Man's weight, and his touch soon found my face. "It's time to feed, pet."

My scratchy throat barely emitted words. "No... I, no... no."

His smile stopped me. "You're dying. Everything inside of you is beginning to decay. The blood will help you through the pain. It will feed the infection and ease you into death. Here." He dipped his finger into a cup, then placed drops of blood on my lips. "Taste it, and you'll see."

Against everything inside of me that remained human, my tongue licked off the blood. The liquid satisfied a visceral, base desire, as if I'd wandered in the desert without water for days before finally being offered a drink. My words echoed out from my dream, despite residing in a living nightmare. "More."

Dark Man set the cup down on a table beside the bed. His hands dove under my arms, and he lifted me to a sitting position. The cup back in hand, he raised it to my lips. "Drink slowly," he said, and the blood trickled into my mouth. After a few seconds, he pulled the cup away.

I grabbed his hand, desperate for more elixir. Instead of providing it, he brought his mouth against mine. This time, his kiss aroused nerves deep inside, ones I never knew existed. My body came back to life as the paralytic wore off, yet new sensations racked me. Ones a human could never experience.

When he parted from me, his breath warmed my face. I tried to find his lips again, but he withheld himself from me. "You're transforming beautifully, pet. In a few days, you will have been made new."

He allowed me another sip of blood, then lowered me down in the bed. "I will be back soon to feed from you again. I'll bring you more blood then." A loving kiss on my forehead, and he disappeared from my view.

I nuzzled my cheek into the pillow and shut my eyes. Seeking to replace the comfort of Dark Man with the blanket, I pulled the fabric tighter against my chest.

"You can't leave me now."

Distress boiled in my gut as Mr. Smith's voice rattled my soul. This wasn't me. I was a chronicler, not a blood seeker. I hadn't left my family and friends behind – my career and entire life – to ingest blood from another and find warmth in Dark Man's dangerous seduction.

"Maybe I've been trying to deny that I feel anything for you, and that's not working for me anymore."

Unbidden tears escaped my eyes as reality set in. Whatever inside of me that remained human silently cried out for Mr. Smith. I had also denied any emotion toward him outside of irritation and contempt. Anything to hold him beyond arm's length. I wished I hadn't done that so many times.

But, now... I was lost. Lost to him, lost to myself. In no time at all, nothing of that woman would remain. I would become a monster for him to slay. Maybe, I already was. I let my tears flow as I drifted back to sleep.

Chapter Thirty-two

Pain wracked my midsection, waking me from dreamless sleep. My arms wrapped around my stomach, and my knees raised to my chest in a fetal position. I squeezed my eyes shut, willing away the torturous, sharp cramps that seized me.

Another set of footsteps approached the bed, but they did not belong to Dark Man. A figure neared the bed, and I opened my tear-filled eyes to see the silhouette of a woman, possibly the one who had been in my room earlier. I had forgotten about her and the other two blood seekers. Had she never left?

Her body sat next to me on the bed, and I rolled over to face her. My eyes narrowed, my head shook ever-so-slightly. *Hallucinations must be common in my state*, I thought. *Or else, I'm in a dream.*

But, as she spoke, her words reinforced that she was there. That she was real. "You have no idea how envious I am right now," she said.

"What... what are you doing here, Liz?" I asked, still not quite believing my eyes. The pain lifted from my abdomen and settled in my heart. Brent, and now *Liz*? What world had Mr. Smith brought me into?

"You haven't figured it out yet, have you?" She sighed and crossed her arms, demonstrating her impatience.

I thought about all our time together, all the laughter, memories. How we'd encourage each other or hold each other up during bad moments. From the time we met, we had been inseparable. Never once had she exhibited any blood seeker behavior. She didn't smell like one, either. "But, you're not a..." The words seemed too strange to utter, but I managed them anyway. "You're not a blood seeker."

"I'm a companion," she said. "I was tasked to find you and stay with you in case you were called as a chronicler."

"You can't be." My mind wandered to Mr. Smith's explanation of a companion's role. "You... you let them feed on you?"

"Of course, I do. You've experienced it now." She leaned over and clucked her tongue. "Better than the best sex, isn't it? And, speaking of sex—"

"But, you can't be a companion. You're my best friend. We spend so much time together, and we..." I remembered our meeting in the coffee shop. How she just so happened to have a free spot at her table and invited me over. Could it be that our meeting wasn't accidental? That her bumping into me was part of a farce that shifted into a fast, one-sided friendship?

"All part of the plan, Mads," she said. "Did you even stop to wonder how they found you at the new hotel after that night stalker spooked you?"

Her betrayal hit me hard – probably what Mr. Smith felt seeing his brother, Brent, as a blood seeker. But, I still had questions. Needed the information should I ever make it back to the complex. "How did you know I'd be called as a chronicler?"

"We didn't. There are hundreds of companions out there, all saddled with the job of befriending an ancestor of a past chronicler. I happened to be the lucky one who found you. Soon enough, I'll be rewarded for it."

"Rewarded?" My stomach churned as a rock sunk inside my gut. I pulled my knees up to my chest once more and clenched my abdomen. The effects of dying, perhaps?

"I'll be like him. Like what you're becoming," she said. "But, don't think for a second you'll take my place by his side. He doesn't care for you, no matter what he says, *pet*." She spat the last word at me in cruel fashion. I'd never heard her so vicious.

Something rose into my throat, bile, vomit... possibly something else. I knew there was only one cure. "Blood," I said. "I need more blood."

"Oh," she said, with mock caring. "You mean this?" She lifted the cup of blood off the table beside me. "I don't think so. I think you're meant to suffer a bit, aren't you? Really feel the effects of death."

Pain gripped my organs, ripping through my torso with a fury like no other. I screamed and clawed at my abdomen, praying for it to stop. "Please!" I begged, before another wail escaped my throat.

She set the cup back down on the table and examined me like a science experiment. "You don't know how lucky you are. Transitioning from life to death like this. Becoming something more – better than human."

"Need... blood..." I could barely get the words past my scratchy throat with the agony seizing my body.

"I think you should be grateful I'm letting you experience the full transition," she said, smiling. "It's so much better when you get to feel everything, don't you think? You should be grateful to—"

"What are you doing?" Dark Man's voice thundered through the room, and he was soon at my bedside. He lifted Liz and shoved her away from me.

"I was just getting her some more blood," Liz said, her repentant voice meek and childlike. "I didn't move fast enough and—"

"How dare you make her wait! Out!"

Without another word, her footsteps scurried out of the room.

Anticipated relief from the anguish filled me as Dark Man sat on the edge of the bed and helped me to sit. The cup touched my lips, and I gulped down the blood. As the liquid flowed down my esophagus, it coated my decaying organs, easing the pain.

He took the cup away from me. "You have to drink slowly," he said. "I'm sorry, pet. I should have never left her with you."

Liz's role in my demise came back to the forefront of my mind, and defeat mocked me once more.

"What do you need?" he asked. "Anything you ask shall be yours."

"Drain me," I whispered, tears flooding my eyes. "End my life."

"You wish for that now," he said, his fingers tangled in my hair, "but not for long."

My heart heavy, I could only think of one other thing. "Then, drink from me. Paralyze me again so I don't feel this slow death."

"Not for a couple more hours. We can't let the virus move too quickly through your body."

My requests denied, I said, "Please don't let her in here again. I can't bear the pain."

"She will be punished for her actions," he said. "But, we need her blood to feed you. Once your transition is complete, she will be sent to another nest far away from here, and she will become food for them. You won't have to worry about her ever again."

If becoming a blood seeker was my fate, at least Liz would face the consequences for her part in it. I'd have to find satisfaction in that.

"I have to leave you, but I will return shortly. Then, I'll stay with you until you are one of us."

The thought of being alone again terrified me, but I also wanted Dark Man to leave. I slipped back down on the bed, under the warmth of the blanket, and watched him retreat. Between Brent, Liz, and my impending death, this nightmare could not get much worse.

An explosion racked the house, shaking the bed. At first, I thought it to be an earthquake, but the nearing sounds of battle painted a new picture in my mind. *Mr. Smith*. He had come for me, though too late. The idea of him seeing me like this... He'd have no choice but to take my head.

I expected Dark Man to rush in and steal me away, but he never came. Minute after minute passed, shifting into what seemed like hours. Maybe everyone had perished, and I would be left to the whimsical throes of death.

When someone entered my room, I sucked in my breath and tried to stave off the growing aching of my body. Mr. Smith's face appeared above me, concern cinching his features as he took in the sight of me. He checked my skin where Dark Man had feasted and shook his head.

I grimaced and clenched my teeth against the pain. I needed more blood, and fast. But, who would feed me now?

"Kill me," I said. "I'm infected."

"Never," he said. "There's got to be another way."

"You don't have a choice. I need... I need more blood."

He fumbled with a knife and slashed at one of the wounds on his arm. "Then, take mine." He lowered his forearm to my lips.

I grasped his arm with both hands and reluctantly drank from him as the tears raced from my eyes, crossing my temples and soaking into my hair. Remembering Dark Man's warnings not to drink too quickly, I slowed myself and released Mr. Smith from my mouth.

He lifted the bottom of his shirt and wiped my lips. "Let's get you out of here."

"No," I said. "You have to kill me. I can't stay like this."

His palm cupped my cheek. "We will find a way to fix this. I don't care how long it takes."

The firmness of his tone convinced me, and I nodded. He tucked the blanket under me, lifted me from the bed, and cradled me in his arms. He carried me through what I thought was my tomb, avoiding the corpses of blood seekers along the way. When he laid me down in the back of an SUV and told someone to drive, I closed my eyes and allowed myself to sleep peacefully.

Chapter Thirty-three

The café where I first met Mr. Smith a million years ago was a most comforting sight, despite having shared time with Liz there. As I wandered to the back room, where Mr. Smith had come into my life, I smiled at his figure – this time, unbound – sitting at our table.

Realizing we were in another shared dream, I understood that he had truly found me and taken me away from Dark Man. That hadn't been a dream. My questions for Mr. Smith bounded out of my mouth. "How did you find me?" I asked, standing at the edge of the table. "How did you even know where to look?"

He glanced down at the white, paper tablecloth, a child caught in the act. "I placed a tracker in one of your shoes."

The revelation didn't faze me. As Keira had said, he was quite stealthy. The old me would have ranted and let anger take control. But, I should have known he would do something like that to keep tabs on me. Just in case. Besides, I was safe. Alive. I could not be angry at him for saving my life, again.

I lowered myself into the seat across from him, and we spent a few moments in warm silence, staring into each other's eyes. I no longer experienced irritation around him, nor any form of contempt. In the room, dying at Dark Man's hands, I had come to accept my feelings for Mr. Smith, whatever they were and wherever they might lead.

"You look good," he said, breaking the stillness between us. "You have no idea how scared I was when I found you."

"I'm sure this isn't what I look like outside of this dream," I said.

The corner of his mouth tweaked upward. *"You're looking better out there, too."*

"How am I still alive? Or, am I still alive?"

"You are," he said. *"You've not breached death yet, and you won't."*

Half-alive, half-dead. In a perpetual state of dying. *"How long has it been?"*

"The doctor induced the coma a week ago. We had to keep you under until we knew how to save you."

Hope swelled in my chest. *"And, did you? Save me?"*

His smile fell, crushing my spirits. *"You're alive, but you'll always have the virus inside of you."*

The revelation brought back every bit of fear I experienced with Dark Man. *"I don't understand. How am I still alive then?"*

"It took time to find something to substitute for a cure. Every day, we've fed you half a pint of blood, and you've improved in your condition. We think that, soon, the virus will weaken and you won't need blood daily. But, you'll still require it on occasion – most likely weekly – so the virus doesn't take control and kill you."

I leaned back in my seat and let out a heavy breath. I didn't want to live as a blood seeker, but this almost seemed worse. A time bomb inside of me that could go off if it wasn't fed. What if something changed in the future and the transformation into a blood seeker continued? Completed?

From across the table, Mr. Smith's hand landed on mine. *"You're going to be fine, Madison. There's nothing to worry about."*

But, I still worried.

"If something happens and I turn—"

"Nothing will happen," he said.

"If it does, I want you to be the one to end my life. It's only right."

Much like before the mission, when I had asked him to promise me the same thing, he hesitated.

"Promise me, Spencer."

He squeezed my hand and said, *"I want to go somewhere else. Somewhere more pleasant."*

I narrowed my eyes, wondering what he meant. In a blink, the scenery around me changed, and we stood on the balcony at the complex. The sun crowned the mountains, just as it had the first night he took me there.

I wandered toward the edge, halting at the railing. *"It is much nicer* here," I said wistfully, gazing at the beautiful scene before me.

Mr. Smith stepped up beside me, close enough that our arms brushed against each other. "Much better," he said.

"How do we keep finding each other in a dream?" I asked, afraid of the answer.

His shoulders heaved with several deep breaths. "I don't mind so much," he said.

The words floated around us, and in that moment, I wished I could read his mind. Taking a chance, I turned my body to face him, and I slipped my hand around his upper arm.

He also turned, stepping an inch closer so our bodies collided, but he didn't move beyond that. I stared up at him, into the eyes I'd come to adore, and lost myself in the reflection of his soul. Still, he remained static, no matter how much I silently begged him to do something.

I remembered our previous kiss – the passion and anger combined – and realized he wasn't about to make that mistake again. Yet, I was also too afraid of... everything.

"Madison—"

Lifting up on my tiptoes, I reached for his face, silencing him. My hand caressed the stubble across his cheek, and he finally lowered his mouth to mine. As the kiss intensified, waves of emotion crashed into me. I pressed into him, letting him know in that moment that I was his, despite knowing that it would not go any further than this. Not in a dream, at least. Maybe not even outside of one.

But, the kiss continued, neither of us able to take enough from each other. The man had saved my life, more than a few times, yet it had nothing to do with how I saw him. There was something more between us – it had been there since the moment we met in the bookstore, though unrecognized by either of us. Or, maybe we did see it, but chose to push it away. No matter how it started, no matter how we reacted to it, this was how I wanted it at that moment. In his arms, driven over the brink by his lips, his hands...

"Spencer."

The familiar voice broke through the dream, and suddenly, I stood in my bedroom at the complex, no longer lip-locked with Mr. Smith. I looked around to find him leaning back in a recliner, one that had been moved in my room since the last time I saw it. His eyes opened, he breathed deeply, and he stared at the door as he came into consciousness.

"Hey, Spence," Keira said. "Sorry to wake you."

He shook his head, as if gathering his bearings. His gaze traveled to my bed, and I followed it. I slept quietly, a ventilator in my mouth and an IV connected to my arm. There were other things, machines, tubes, equipment I didn't recognize. I realized that while Keira had broken through my shared dream with Mr. Smith, I was still lost in that world, but somehow able to see and hear their interaction.

"It's okay," he said. "What's up?"

"You should really eat something," she said. "You've been asleep for a while now."

He glanced back at my form on the bed.

"I know you don't want to leave her," Keira said, "but I can sit with her while you eat."

"Do you mind just bringing me something in here?"

Keira crossed the room and stood over him. "You've barely left her room since we brought her back."

"And, I don't plan on it until she wakes up." He rose from the chair. "Tell you what. If you can bring me something to eat, I'll stay here with her." He walked to my bedside and took a seat in an empty chair next to my body. Staring down at me, he asked, "Is it time for the doctor to take more blood?"

"Spence, you can't keep up like this. I know you want to make sure she's good, but you don't have to be the only one giving her blood. Garrett is also compatible—"

"No," he said.

"It's too much blood," she said. "The doctor said—"

"It's going to be my blood and mine alone. I don't want anyone else having to do this. Besides, she'll be awake soon."

"What makes you say that?" Keira asked.

He smiled at me, and his tongue wet his lips as if he still tasted me on them. The gesture set my heart into an irregular beat, and a beep on one of the monitors indicated it.

His smile grew as he stared down at me. "Oh, I have a feeling it'll be real soon."

Chapter Thirty-four

Five weeks later...

The feather pen dipped into the black of the inkwell. I wondered how much to shake off the tip before touching it to paper, but gave it a try anyway. Black ink soaked into the paper, not too heavy, but enough to see the words I wrote: *The Chronicler*.

I replaced the quill in its resting place and smiled at the title of my first chronicle. Enough time had passed for my wounds – inside and out – to heal. Now, I had to record the history of my first mission. I decided to begin with how I was called into the life, knowing it might help others in the future through those first few uncertain days after they, too, were called.

My blood intake was down to half a pint once a week, and Mr. Smith continued to supply the blood that entered my body. He refused to allow anyone else to help. He claimed me to be his responsibility and his failure that I had been taken by Dark Man. Since I no longer had the feeding tube I'd had while in the medically-induced coma, I had to drink his blood the old fashioned way. Though much more sterile than when I first fed from him – first taken from him by the doctor, then cleaned and prepared for consumption – it was still something we shared together, privately, and in a closed room. We never spoke during the sessions, but it worked for us.

Not too long after I awoke, I learned that Dark Man had escaped the blood seekers. Something about the revelation didn't surprise me. Though his ability to infiltrate my thoughts had faded, he still seemed present in my life – and I knew he could also feel me in the world. Mr. Smith figured that he wouldn't show up for a long time, if ever. He had a nest to rebuild, and another complex had taken over tracking him for the time being.

Rich had been the only night stalker to perish during the battle at the factory. After I finished my first chronicle, I planned on learning more about him so I could record his life in a separate book. He deserved much more than just a brief mention.

After an emotionally torturous battle, Mr. Smith had taken his brother's head at the factory, though it hadn't affected him as much as I would have thought. He had already believed his brother dead, so nothing had changed for him from before to after the mission – at least, that was what he outwardly claimed. Something told me not to believe him.

From the moment I awoke from my medically-induced coma, Liz resumed haunting me. Moments of our friendship – or what I thought was our friendship – entered my mind every so often. How much had she faked during our time together? For the sake of sanity, I tried to believe that not all of it had been a farce, though I knew better.

I had been caught off-guard when Keira told me Liz survived the ambush of the house I had been held in. Garrett and Andre had captured her, and she was quickly shipped to an overseas complex for interrogation. I wanted to know all about her, but hesitated to ask. Torturing myself over her deception would not do me any good in my quest to recover from the past, especially when I had to live with the consequences of the virus and the knowledge that Dark Man could still find me one day.

The door to the Chronicle Library opened, and I shook my head. Mr. Smith – as I had resumed calling him from the moment I woke up – never failed to interrupt me at the worst possible times. Since the one while in my coma, we'd experienced no more shared dreams, nor had we discussed them. We remained friendly, with no animosity between us. He still trained me in the gym, still answered my questions when learning, and kept preparing me for my future as the chronicler. We also still took jabs at each other at every possible turn, though they were always out of affection and no longer filled with hostility. So many times, the words had been on my lips – possibly his as well – but we never once spoke about the kiss we shared in the dream. I was okay with that. I don't think I ever expected anything from him, no matter how much I thought about it – maybe even wanted it.

"How are you feeling today?" he asked as he neared my desk.

"Stronger than ever," I said.

"Good." He turned the page in front of me and read it. "*The Chronicler.*"

"I decided it's time to jot down my first chronicle."

"Really? And, you're using a quill pen to do it?"

"I'm not that much of a masochist." I laughed and shrugged. "I thought I'd do the first page like the chroniclers of old. The rest of it, I'll type."

"Interesting." He reached across the desk, grabbed the pen, and dipped it in the ink. Before I could protest, he scribbled something on the paper below my words. When he replaced the pen, he rotated the page so I could read it, a triumphant smile beaming on his face.

"*The Chronicler and Mr. Smith.*" I smirked and looked up at him. "Cute. Just had to put yourself in there, huh?"

"Seems fitting," he said. "Well, I suppose I should leave you to it. Uh… don't make me out to be too much of a jerk. If you can help it, that is."

My smile acted as my response. Whether he came across as a jerk would be up to the future chroniclers to decide.

As he walked back toward the hallway leading out of the library, I stopped him. "Wait, Spencer?"

He turned to me, his head lowered, eying me. "Spencer, now, is it?"

I tried to stammer out words, some excuse for deviating from what I always called him, but I couldn't find one. Instead, I said, "I'm not sure how to go about this."

"What do you mean?"

"I mean, how do I write this chronicle? Is it a book form like a memoir? Is it done in journal form? Or, do I write it like a reporter telling a story? I've read other chronicles for ideas, but I'm not sure what the best way is to approach it."

He nodded and thought for a moment. "I think the best way for you to do it is like what you writers typically do. In whatever way it decides to come out, write it down exactly like that."

And, so I did.

###

Mr. Smith's Hunting Playlist

Enter Sandman – Metallica
Bodies – Drowning Pool
The Kill – Thirty Seconds to Mars
I Stand Alone – Godsmack
Before I Forget – Slipknot
Blow Me Away (feat Valora) – Breaking Benjamin
You're Going Down – Sick Puppies
Animal I Have Become – Three Days Grace
Lights Out – Breaking Benjamin
Time Bomb - Godsmack
Life is Beautiful – Sixx:A.M.
Renegade – Styx
(Don't Fear) The Reaper – Blue Öyster Cult
Metalingus – Alter Bridge
Bat Country – Avenged Sevenfold
Awake and Alive – Skillet

Author's Note

This all started as a dream.

No, seriously. In March 2017, I woke up one morning after watching too much *Supernatural* and remembered wisps of a fabulous dream starring Jensen Ackles (Dean Winchester) and myself. It had to do with secret orders and slaying monsters... all those fun things that I really enjoy. Plus, Dean Winchester.

In March 2018, I put fingers to keyboard and started typing out *The Chronicler and Mr. Smith*. Although it was nothing like that dream, it ended up being a journey I would never forget. The book mixed bits of *Supernatural* with bits of *Assassin's Creed* and, of course, I added in my own little fun twists.

The title began as *The Chronicler* and changed to *The Chronicler and Mr. Smith* after the cover was photographed. That's when Mr. Smith just wouldn't stop telling me that he had a much bigger role in this thing that I ever thought. Turns out, he was right.

The original score written by my son, Christian Goscha and performed by him and David Bryant, is one of the best songs I've ever heard. And, I may be a little biased (my son, my "other son," and my book), but yeah, it's pretty damn awesome. When I heard the song the first time, I knew exactly what to title it. I played around with a few words before coming up with *Vengeance Divided (Mr. Smith's Theme)*. The song sounds like Mr. Smith's internal debate about his life, his role in his brother's death, and how to handle it. It's something we never hear about firsthand in the book (since the book is in Madison's point of view), but there are hints to his struggles. That Christian captured it so perfectly in his song is amazing to me.

As for the blood seekers themselves, I love creatures and monsters of all kinds, but I really like to make up things that are unique – as you probably guessed from *Conduit* and

Chrysalis. Since creating a whole new monster is difficult enough, I ended up rolling with the whole vampire/zombie with demon origins thing. I'd always wanted to write about vampires (they are *scary*, not *glittery!*), and zombies have fascinated me since childhood. I had just written about demons in *Chrysalis*, but I loved the idea of my monsters having Biblical origins, so I went with it. I think it worked out okay.

And, finally, the question that is on every reader's mind who has reached out to me after finishing the book: Will there be more Mads and Mr. Smith? The answer is a very definite "yes." This book has been an incredibly fun journey, one that I want to take again and very soon. There is so much more story to tell with lots of monsters yet to be introduced. Oh, yes, there are more than blood seekers out there, and I cannot wait to introduce them to your imaginations and, hopefully, nightmares.

Thank you so much to all my readers for making this and every book I write both a possibility and a reality. Without you, I wouldn't have much to say. Until next time…

Angie Martin

More by Angie Martin

Chrysalis

Winner ~ Honorable Mention for Paranormal Fiction in the 2018 Reader's Favorite International Book Awards

Sheriff Peter Holbrook leads a simple life watching over the residents of Nowhere, Kansas, where the most noteworthy crimes are dognappings and brawls at the local tavern. He's always had an inherent fear of the gray – the yearly spring storms that plague the area. As the gray descends on Nowhere, a mysterious woman crashes her car just outside city limits. The tattooed stranger may not remember who she is, but Peter instantly feels a connection with her.

But, the girl's appearance isn't the oddest event. Unusual behavior from the townsfolk, cattle mutilation, and death soon follow. Peter believes they are related, but only has his instincts and prophetic ramblings from his deceased mother. As the mysteries and bodies pile up, he turns to the stranger for help in hopes to save his sleepy town.

The Boys Club

Winner ~ Silver Medal for Suspense Fiction in the 2014 Reader's Favorite International Book Awards

Growing up a homeless juvenile delinquent left its mark on Gabriel Logan. He lived a throwaway existence until a former FBI agent recruited him for a fringe organization for boys like him, ones who could operate outside the law for the sake of justice. As an adult, he sets an example for the others and is slated to take over their group, until his work results in the murder of his pregnant wife.

Going through the motions of everyday life, Logan does only what's required of him with one goal in mind: kill Hugh Langston, the man responsible for his wife's death. When he's handed the opportunity to bring Langston down, he jumps at the chance, but the job will challenge him more than anything in the past. Not only does he have to save Langston's daughter from her father's hit list, but the job seems to have come to them a little too easily. Logan must find a way to not only rescue the one woman who can take down his biggest enemy, but also look into the men he trusts most to discover which one of them is betraying The Boys Club.

Conduit

Bestseller on Amazon US and Amazon UK
Winner ~ Gold Medal for Paranormal Fiction in the 2014 Reader's Favorite International Book Awards

How do you hide from a killer when he's in your mind?

Emily Monroe conceals her psychic gift from the world, but her abilities are much too strong to keep hidden from an equally gifted killer. A savvy private investigator, she discreetly uses her psychic prowess to solve cases. When the police ask her to assist on a new case, she soon learns the killer they seek is not only psychic, but is targeting her.

The killer wants more than to invade her mind; he wants her. Believing they are destined for each other, he uses his victims as conduits to communicate with her, and she hears their screams while they are tortured. She opens her mind to help the victims, but it gives him a portal that he uses to lure her to him. With the killer taking over her mind, she must somehow stop him before she becomes his next victim.

False Security

Rachel Thomas longs for normalcy, but if she stops running, she could die…or worse. Chased by a past that wishes to imprison her, haunted by dreams that seek to destroy her, Rachel finds solace in a love she could not predict. A love she cannot deter.

Mark Jacobson is the man who never needed love. He has his bookstore, his bachelorhood, and his freedom. In the moment he meets Rachel, he is swept into a world he didn't know existed. One filled with the purest of love. One filled with betrayal, lies, and murder.

Now Rachel and Mark are forced to face her past. The truth may kill them both.

False Hope

Rachel Thomas has spent the last four years running from her past. Forced into Witness Protection and exiled from the rest of the world, she manages to survive, but still lives each day in fear of being found again while trying to overcome her emotional wounds and past misdeeds as a criminal.

Mark Jacobson wants nothing more than to provide Rachel with the normal life she's always wanted. Dealing with his own scars and helpless to change their situation, he struggles to maintain his tenuous hold on his anger.

To find peace in a world she can share with Mark, Rachel agrees to help the FBI bring down all those who are after her. While the FBI believes she and Mark are safe, they are being watched closer than ever before. And, someone is ready to bring her home for good.

Shadows

From the bestselling, award-winning author of "Conduit" and "The Boys Club" comes a collection of short stories designed to illicit chills and keep you up at night. Shadows takes readers on a thrill ride through tales of hospital rooms and haunted houses, introducing everything from serial killers to the boogeyman. Includes "The First Step" written with bestselling author Marisa Oldham.

the three o'clock in the morning sessions

"the three o'clock in the morning sessions" is a poetry collection of works written over the span of almost fifteen years. This book also contains two short stories, "the door" and "brief love". All of the works deal with lost love or unrequited loves.

About Angie Martin

Angie is an award-winning, lifelong writer and firmly believes that words flow through her veins. She lives in Calimesa, California with her husband, two cats, and beloved dog. She also has two sons paving their own way in the world. She grew up in Wichita, Kansas and has lived all over the United States. Her work reflects her background in criminal justice and her love of Midwest life.

She has released six novels in the suspense/thriller, paranormal/supernatural thriller, and horror genres. She also has a poetry/short story collection and has contributed short stories to multiple anthologies.

"Conduit" won the Gold Medal for Paranormal Fiction in the 2014 Readers' Favorite International Book Awards. "The Boys Club" won the Silver Medal for Suspense Fiction in the 2015 Readers' Favorite International Book Awards. It was also voted as one of the 2014-15 Top 50 Self-Published Books Worth Reading (ReadFree.ly). Chrysalis was also awarded Honorable Mention for Paranormal Fiction in the 2018 Reader's Favorite International Book Awards, voted one of the 2018 Top 50 Self-Published Books Worth Reading (ReadFree.ly), and a finalist and semifinalist in other highly respected competitions. All of her works have won additional readers' choice and blog choice awards.

. Website: www.angiemartinbooks.com
Fan Group: www.facebook.com/groups/angiesconduits
Facebook: www.facebook.com/authorangiemartin
Twitter: www.twitter.com/zmbchica
Angie's books: bit.ly/thrillingbooks

One Last Thing...

Thanks for reading! If you enjoyed this book, I'd be very grateful if you would post a short review on Amazon and/or BookBub. Your support really does make a difference, and I read all the reviews personally so I can get your feedback. Thank you again for your support!

Made in the USA
Columbia, SC
09 February 2022